THE LOST ONES

THE LOST ONES

The Moonwind Mysteries

JOHAN RUNDBERG
TRANSLATED BY EVA APELQVIST

This is a work of fiction. Names, characters, organizations, places, events, and incidents are either products of the author's imagination or are used fictitiously. Any resemblance to actual persons, living or dead, or actual events is purely coincidental.

Text copyright © 2021, 2025 by Johan Rundberg
Translation copyright © 2025 by Eva Apelqvist
All rights reserved.

No part of this book may be reproduced, or stored in a retrieval system, or transmitted in any form or by any means, electronic, mechanical, photocopying, recording, or otherwise, without express written permission of the publisher.

Previously published as *Dödsängeln* by Natur & Kultur in Sweden in 2021. Translated from Swedish by Eva Apelqvist. First published in English by Amazon Crossing Kids in collaboration with Amazon Crossing in 2025.

Published by Amazon Crossing Kids, New York, in collaboration with Amazon Crossing

www.apub.com

Amazon, Amazon Crossing, and all related logos are trademarks of Amazon.com, Inc., or its affiliates.

ISBN-13: 9781662525940 (hardcover)
ISBN-13: 9781662525957 (paperback)
ISBN-13: 9781662525568 (digital)

Cover design and illustration by Edward Bettison Ltd.

Printed in the United States of America

First edition

THE
LOST ONES

CHAPTER 1

Stockholm, Sweden, 1880

The sun is high in the sky, and in the courtyard of the Public Children's Home, the shadows are so short that even a mouse wouldn't be able to find relief near the walls of the building. A drop of sweat runs down Mika's forehead, and she makes a face when the salt stings her eye. She grabs a handful of straw from the sack and shoves it into the mattress cover. The sharp sticks scratch the skin on her forearm. The Department of Health is coming for an inspection, and Amelia, the houseparent of the orphanage, has decided that all the mattresses must be restuffed. Mika ties the mattress together. Then she reaches for another one and shakes out the old straw. It is full of black dots: mouse poop and dead bedbugs. Even though the latrine was emptied recently, a sweet-and-sour stench permeates the yard.

Not that it's better anywhere else in Stockholm; the heat wave of the past few weeks does not discriminate between rich and poor. The horse manure in the streets, the butchers' meat scraps, the putrid backyard latrines—the smells mingle and rise like a thick vapor throughout the city. The ruthless cold of last winter feels like another life.

A sharp stick pokes Mika under the nail and she swears between clenched teeth. If only Rufus were here to help. But Rufus has something important to do, something that he refused to tell her about. *If he's gone swimming, I'll kill him,* Mika thinks, and pulls at her dress, irritated. It's glued to her back. The thought of Strömmen Bay's cool water gives her goose bumps. Maybe Amelia will let her sneak away for a quick dip when her work is done, to rinse away the sweat and old straw.

Her daydream comes to an end when a hard knock rattles the gate to the courtyard. She hears Ossian's voice calling out from inside the children's home.

"The police are here!"

Mika immediately drops what she's doing. Fear courses through her body when she notices that the lock from the gate is sitting on the ground by the wooden fence. Her carelessness means that she now has only seconds. With a leap, she's on top of the water tank; then she pulls herself up onto the outhouse roof. From there, she steadies herself, then jumps over to the courtyard building. Mika has practiced this escape route many times, but she still trips when she lands and falls flat on the scalding-hot tar paper. From the yard comes a bang when the gate opens. Mika's heart thunders in her chest as she gets up on her feet. She starts climbing down the downspout, her dress heavy with sticky tar. Next to the eastern chimney on the orphanage roof is a coiled rope. Mika plans to let herself down behind the building. From there, it will be easy to disappear into the alleys around Hötorget Square. *If I don't get shot first,* she thinks, and despite the heat, a cold shiver runs up her spine. Hanging there on the side of the building, she's an easy target.

But there is no shot. Instead, she hears a familiar voice from the courtyard.

"Where's the fire, Ragamuffin?"

For a moment, Mika hangs there between the second and third floor; then she loosens her grip on the downspout and slides back onto the roof of the building. Her pulse is still quick when she walks toward the edge. Down in the yard is Constable Valdemar Hoff from the Criminal Investigations Department. From this angle, he looks no bigger than an orphan. Even though most orphans don't have a red nose and a full beard.

"Can't you just knock like a normal person," Mika hisses. "Did you have to bring the entire gate down?"

"I didn't bring down any gate," Valdemar objects, shading his eyes with his hand. "Come down so I can talk to you."

"I can hear you just fine from here," Mika replies, still irritated at having been frightened. "Nobody saw you coming, right? And weren't you supposed to stay away from the orphanage? Wasn't that the agreement?"

Valdemar sighs. "Fair enough," he says. "But the investigation into your involvement with the explosion at the jail has been closed."

Mika feels her legs weaken and she wobbles, very close to the edge of the roof.

"Say that again," she says.

"You heard me," Valdemar says. "If you plan to tumble off the edge, I would like to point out that your mattress pile is a little too far away."

Mika jumps down and lands with a thud on top of the empty water tank. She walks up to Valdemar, who raises his eyebrows.

"What happened?" he asks. "Did you cheat at cards?"

Mika realizes how she must look, sticky from top to bottom with wood tar and her hair full of straw. She pretends she didn't hear Valdemar's question.

"Is the case closed then?" she asks suspiciously. "The police aren't going to solve it?"

"The actual explosion is still being looked into," Valdemar replies. "But the investigators cannot figure out why somebody with access to explosives would try to free an orphan girl who had been arrested. This is why the police now view the two events as unrelated—they think the strike just happened to hit the cell you were in."

"So, what happens now?" Mika asks.

"According to the authorities, you are a child thief without a surname," Valdemar replies. "Your disappearance is simply not important enough to investigate. Besides, there was enough blood in that place that it was deemed pointless to continue the search. According to the police, your body is most likely at the bottom of the Strömmen. So . . ."

He throws his hands in the air. "You're free."

Mika snorts. "Free," she repeats scornfully.

"You know what I mean," Valdemar says. "You don't have to worry about the police searching for you anymore, here or at the Chapel. On the other hand, you might want to avoid greeting the policemen who arrested you if you happen to see them in the street."

He slowly looks Mika over, then adds:

"Even though I doubt they would recognize you."

A wave of relief washes over Mika. Almost three months have passed since she was wrongly arrested for the theft of the Magatama gemstone and Tekla freed her by blowing a hole in her cell wall at the jail. Ever since then, Mika has been on guard, always with an escape route ready, sneaking around close to the buildings like a skittish animal on the lookout for the next cavity to hide in. It finally feels like she has been let out of jail for real.

"Do you happen to know where Tekla is?" Valdemar continues.

Mika shakes her head. "Why are you asking?"

"Attacking a police station is a serious crime," Valdemar explains. "Not to mention embarrassing for those in charge. The explosives used in the attack have been analyzed, and it's not dynamite but a substance called gelignite. It's a brand-new product, not yet available to the public. The investigators believe that the guilty party has connections to Alfred Nobel's factories. The same factory that had an explosion two years ago."

Mika doesn't tell him what she's thinking, but she knows that both Tekla and one of the other members of the Girls' gang, Nitro-Nellie, have worked at the Nobel factory in Vinterviken.

"I prefer to stay away from Tekla, but I need to talk to her," Valdemar continues. "She has helped both of us, but the noose is tightening. For her own sake, she needs to avoid blowing up any more buildings."

"I haven't seen her since that night at the jail," Mika says truthfully. "I don't even know if she's alive."

"If you see her, tell her that it would be nice if she came to find me."

Valdemar takes off his hat and wipes sweat from his forehead. Mika suddenly notices that something is different. Valdemar has had a haircut, there are no rips or tears in his shirt or coat, and he doesn't smell of horse or schnapps.

"What happened to you?" she exclaims. "Are you going to a wedding?"

Valdemar looks surprised; then he laughs.

"Nope, I haven't been to a wedding since my own," he says. "I've been given a new case and need to visit one of the nicer neighborhoods. I just wanted to stop on the way and give you the news about the investigation."

Mika is burning with curiosity, but she resists asking more questions. The mattress pile by the wall looms high, like a lice-infested mountain; Valdemar has his job to do, and she has hers. Mika holds back a sigh and pulls a sticky piece of straw from her hair.

Valdemar turns his face to the sun, as if to determine the time. Then he looks at Mika again.

"Do you want to come?"

CHAPTER 2

In the King's Garden, women's parasols sway like dandelions in a field. Boys and girls from the nice neighborhoods eat their box lunches in the shade of the willow trees. And by the water-spouting swans on Molin's fountain, a line has formed, with people looking to cool off in the heat. Mika walks next to Valdemar, feeling the stickiness of the wood tar between her toes in her boots. But her face and hands have been scrubbed clean, her dress has been changed, and her hair has been put up in a bun that appears tidy if you don't look too carefully.

"It was generous of your houseparent to let you come with me," Valdemar says. "I'm afraid she would have bashed my head in if I had asked her myself. That's why I used the gate to the courtyard."

"Hmm . . ."

Mika tries to figure out how she can avoid lying. Because she didn't actually ask permission to leave the children's home; she just left. She doesn't usually do that. But she had a feeling that Amelia would say no, because she hates Valdemar like the plague.

"So, you get to investigate real cases again?" Mika asks, changing the subject. "I thought you were still chasing pickpockets in Norrbro."

Valdemar grins. "Things have changed since you last saw me," he says. "I'm not exactly my bosses' favorite, but they have a little more faith in me since I handed them the Magatama gem."

Mika remembers the newspaper article that Amelia read at breakfast a few days after the events in the spring. It said that an anonymous police officer had found the invaluable precious stone that the adventurer Nordenskiöld had been given as a gift by Japan's emperor, but that had disappeared in the events surrounding a gala dinner at the House of Nobility. An international band of art thieves was believed to be behind the theft, even though neither thieves nor client had been identified. But thanks to the heroic police officer, the precious stone was back where it belonged, in a display cabinet at the Palace library. The king himself had praised the Stockholm police for a job well done.

"*You* should have been the one thanked by the king," Valdemar says.

Mika doesn't reply. What is she supposed to say? They both know the idea of the king thanking an orphan is ridiculous. Besides, Mika's just happy that neither Ossian nor Kristina—the other orphans involved—was harmed or sent to a correctional facility as a result of that night.

"What kind of case did you get?" she asks.

"A girl has disappeared," Valdemar replies. "A few years older than you."

"Children disappear all the time," Mika points out.

"I hardly need to tell you that some lives are valued more than others," Valdemar says. "And this girl is not just anybody. Or rather, her father is not just anybody. Have you heard of Charles Douglas?"

Mika shakes her head.

"He's a well-known businessman in the textile industry," Valdemar explains. "Owns a few of the biggest factories in town. He contacted the police yesterday and asked for help finding his daughter. That's all I know."

At the northern end of Blasieholmstorg Square is a magnificent stone building, five stories high. The glass front door is framed by two ornamental falcons spreading their wings.

"When we get inside—" Valdemar begins.

"I will stay close to you and not reply when people address me," Mika interrupts. "I know."

At first, Valdemar looks a little surprised; then he fixes his eyes on Mika.

"When we do investigations or visit crime scenes together, your presence always risks being called into question," he says, looking serious. "And if somebody demands that you leave, I can't object. The only way to do this is if they believe that you're a harmless errand girl. That's why it's important that you don't talk back at me when other people can hear it."

Valdemar takes off his hat and runs a hand through his hair; then he bangs so hard on the front door that the glass planes rattle.

"You need to learn how to knock," Mika quips.

"What did I just tell you?" Valdemar mutters.

"We're still outside," Mika points out.

"Well, yes, but it's . . ."

Valdemar quiets when a shadow moves behind the glass panes. The door opens and an older man dressed in a butler's uniform appears in the doorway.

"My name is Constable Valdemar Hoff. I have an appointment with Mr. Douglas."

Without a word, the butler lets them in. A dazzlingly white marble floor spreads out in front of them like a frozen ocean. Behind a sliding door, they glimpse a large drawing room where maids are setting a table. Mika feels the girls' eyes on her when she and Valdemar pass through the hallway and follow the butler up a staircase. The magnificent surroundings remind Mika of her visits to the home of the Carstenius family, a wealthy family that also lives on Arsenalsgatan. She immediately feels like she's shrinking, becoming an insect that crawls up through a crack in the floor and scurries across the open space, leaving dirty footprints behind. For a moment, she almost thinks she can hear the squelching of wood tar in her boots. She can tell that the surroundings are affecting Valdemar too. In a house like this, clean clothes or an attempt at combing your hair won't help. In the light of the hallway chandeliers, Valdemar looks as disheveled as usual, as if somebody has squeezed a bear into a pair of pants and trained it to walk on its hind legs.

At the very end of the hallway is a corner room with a view of the square. By the window stand a tall man in a suit and a woman in a green dress. The butler knocks carefully on the door.

"Constable Hoff," he announces. Then he turns to Valdemar and says quietly, "Mr. and Mrs. Douglas."

Valdemar barely has time to open his mouth to introduce himself before Mr. Douglas points at Mika with the shaft of his pipe.

"Do the police usually bring their children on assignments?"

"The girl is not my child," Valdemar replies tersely. "She helps me with practical matters and will not interfere. Shall we sit down?"

A tense silence descends over the room. Mika lowers her eyes and tries to make herself as invisible as she can. Finally, Mr. Douglas nods and points to an armchair next to the desk.

"Please be seated."

Valdemar sits down and pulls out his notebook, while the Douglases seat themselves on the couch by the fireplace. Mika stands with her back to the wall; in her dark-blue shirt, she practically blends in with the wallpaper.

"I contacted the police because our daughter, Beatrice, has been gone for two days," Mr. Douglas says. "Friday afternoon, she went to the King's Garden to meet some friends. She never returned."

"Three days," Valdemar says, looking up from his notes.

"Excuse me?"

"You said that your daughter has been gone since Friday," Valdemar says. "That means that she has been gone for more than two days. I'm sorry if I get hung up on details, but those details are important in this context."

An irritated wrinkle appears on Mr. Douglas's forehead, but then he nods.

"The constable is right—three days it is, of course."

Mrs. Douglas puts a hand on her husband's arm. "We should have reported Beatrice's disappearance immediately, of course, but we thought there was a natural explanation and that she would return by the weekend."

Valdemar nods.

"Most disappearances have a natural explanation," he says. "Do you know the names of the friends she was going to meet?"

"I'm afraid not," Mrs. Douglas replies. "We have talked to the parents of the children that she usually spends time with in class, but none of her friends were with her on this occasion."

"I'll need the names of those you consider your daughter's closest friends," Valdemar says, passing his notebook across the table to Mr. Douglas, who passes it on to his wife.

Mika notices that nobody is aware of her presence anymore. Carefully, she raises her eyes and looks around the room. On the wall above the fireplace hangs an oil painting of Mr. Douglas. Or perhaps it's a painting of how

Mr. Douglas sees himself. In the painting, he is at least forty pounds lighter than in real life. He has a wide chin and thick, shiny hair. Next to his desk is a serving cart with a humidor for cigars and a few well-filled decanters of cognac.

"That's right. We picked out a photograph that you may use." Mrs. Douglas stands up and pulls out a drawer in the desk. With a stern look, she hands Valdemar an envelope, adding, "We assume that you will handle this investigation discreetly. Neither the photograph nor any other information may under any circumstances reach the newspapers. We want to keep this in the family as much as possible."

"We'll keep this quiet, I assure you," Valdemar says.

He takes out the photograph and intentionally holds it up in front of him so that Mika can see it as well. The picture shows a girl with dark, braided hair and a serious face. With her almond-shaped eyes and distinct nose, Beatrice Douglas does not look very much like either one of her parents.

"She'll turn fifteen in October," Mrs. Douglas adds. "And she still has the same hairstyle, though it may not be as nicely combed as in the picture. My daughter can be a little messy, you see."

"Has anything else of value disappeared from your home?" Valdemar asks, putting the photograph in his notebook.

Mr. Douglas raises his eyebrows. "Not that we noticed. What are you suggesting?"

"Is it possible that your daughter is staying away of her own free will?" Valdemar asks bluntly.

The Douglases exchange a surprised look, as if the thought has never occurred to them.

"My daughter has no reason to run away from her own home," Mrs. Douglas says sharply. "And she is used to a rather high level of comfort, with both a water closet and her own room. Even if she decided to have a little adventure and run out in the woods, she wouldn't be able to stand it for more than a night."

Valdemar looks as kind as his scarred face allows.

"You will have to excuse me if some of my questions seem blunt," he says. "I don't know your daughter the way you do. Might we—I mean, might I be allowed to see her room?"

The irritated wrinkle reappears on Mr. Douglas's forehead. He throws a quick glance at the wall clock and makes a gesture toward the door.

"If you believe that it may be of help in your work."

Mr. Douglas shows them back through the hallway, to the room closest to the stairs. He turns the key and opens the door. Mika stays quiet in the background the entire time. But when she steps over the threshold into Beatrice's room, she cannot help gasping. One wall is entirely covered with built-in bookshelves. On the opposite wall hangs a heavy, gilded mirror. Under the south-facing window is a nicely organized desk, full of wonderful items—pens, inkhorns, and paper in all colors and sizes. Under the bed are a potty and a washbasin. A stuffed toy bear wearing a tiny knit sweater that has bunched-up around the belly lies on a crocheted bedspread. On a side table next to the window is a gilded birdcage with a bright-eyed and colorful finch on a perch. Excited about the sudden visit, the bird flaps its wings and chirps.

Mika is dumbfounded. It is unimaginable that somebody could have an entire room to herself. And what a room at that; Mika has never seen anything like it.

Mrs. Douglas reaches across the bed and rearranges the bear into a sitting position, even strokes its cheek as if it were a child. When she turns to Valdemar, her eyes are shiny with tears.

"As you can see, my daughter lacked for nothing," she says.

Valdemar nods. "That's obvious," he says.

"Unfortunately, Beatrice did not keep a journal," Mrs. Douglas adds. "If you had hoped to find something that might explain her disappearance, I mean."

"I will use the information at hand," Valdemar replies. "Nobody disappears without leaving some sort of trace. Let me talk to your daughter's friends and I'll get in touch as soon as I can."

On their way out, Mika furtively slides her hand over the bedspread.

"Well," Valdemar asks as they walk home across Blasieholmstorg Square. "Did you notice anything in particular?"

Mika thinks for a while, then replies: "It was a play for the galleries."

"A play for the galleries?" Valdemar repeats warily. "You mean they were lying?"

Mika shakes her head.

"Not necessarily," she replies. "But you were. You said that nobody disappears without leaving a trace, but what about Klara Lind? All we know is that she died on the job at the factory, but her death was never confirmed. In fact, it was covered up. And she is far from the only one."

Valdemar's face turns even more red than usual. "What do you mean by that?"

"I don't know. Not yet."

Mika thinks about Beatrice's room and what the Douglases said. Something wasn't right. If she could just put her finger on it.

"I thought of something," she says as they arrive at the intersection with Stallgatan. "What's a water closet?"

Valdemar stops for a moment to pull his pipe from his inner pocket.

"It's a hollow chair made of porcelain," he explains, knocking the tobacco out against the heel of his boot. "The chair is full of water. If Mr. Douglas wakes up in the middle of the night with an urge, he won't have to squeeze his knees together all the way down to the courtyard. Instead, he pees in the water closet, and when he is done, he pulls a little string, and the pee disappears down a pipe."

"You're pulling my leg."

Mika looks so shocked that Valdemar laughs.

"It's true," he assures her and strikes a match on the side of the box. "Close your mouth—a bird might move in."

Before they continue, Mika turns around and looks toward the gray colossus on the other side of the square. So far, all she has is a hunch. But that hunch tells her that it would be safer for Beatrice Douglas if Valdemar finds her before her own family does.

CHAPTER 3

When Mika returns to the children's home, she sneaks through the gate, into the yard. She sighs when she notices that the mattress pile is still there as she left it. Selfishly, she had hoped that Amelia would pass the task on to one of the big kids, but perhaps nobody even noticed that she was gone.

Mika goes inside to change. The orphanage is usually full of life and activity at this time of day, but now nobody is around, and an unusual stillness has settled over the place. At first, Mika thinks that she might have made a mistake about the time; maybe it's already supper. But the kitchen is empty, as is the dining room.

"Hello," she calls out tentatively, but no one answers.

Then she hears a soft buzzing from the great hall. Gingerly, Mika moves along the hallway toward the open door. Every single child from the orphanage is in the great hall, gathered in a big circle. From the middle of the circle, a dark mess of hair sticks up. Mika's curiosity takes over and she elbows her way to the middle to see what's going on. To her surprise, she realizes that the object of curiosity is Rufus. He is unusually well groomed, wearing a shirt and pants without a single hole or stain. But that's not the only strange thing. On his upper body, Rufus is wearing something made from heavy leather that reminds Mika of a farrier's vest. On his back are two metal poles that end in some kind of headrest. The entire contraption is kept in place by two wide leather strips tightened around his chest.

"What's going on?" Mika asks. "And why are you wearing that ugly contraption?"

Rufus turns around with difficulty. The headrest makes it impossible for him to turn his head without moving his entire upper body; he's as stiff as a corpse.

"It's called a corset," he replies patronizingly, as if Mika were a little slow. "It costs more than you can imagine. And I am wearing it because I have been *chosen*."

"Chosen for what?" Mika snorts. "Crucifixion?"

"He's going to be brought to a correctional facility for children," Margit explains.

"And tied down," Axel adds happily.

"Dear me." Amelia sighs, shaking her head. "Since not everybody here seems to understand what's going on, let's go over it one more time."

Amelia explains how Rufus has been selected for a treatment for children with crooked backs. Once a week, a carriage will pick him up at the children's home and take him to an institution for children with physical disabilities. He will be strapped into a traction bed for a few hours, which will stretch his spine. Then he will be brought back home.

"What kind of strange bed do you strap people into?" Mika asks, making a face.

"It looks like a regular bed," Rufus explains enthusiastically. "My head and my feet are strapped down at both ends; then the doctor turns a crank, and my body is stretched out little by little."

"That's how you tortured people in the olden days," Mika points out.

"It is an expensive and fine treatment," Amelia says sternly. "It is a blessing for Rufus to have been selected."

"And this thing," Mika says, pulling at one of the corset's leather straps. "Do you have to wear it every day?"

Rufus tries to nod, but his head is stuck. "At night, mostly. The doctor said it will make me as straight as a board."

Mika feels the stirrings of anger between her temples. She is angry at Rufus, at Amelia, and at the doctors for promising a bunch of hogwash. She wants to tell Rufus that he is fine the way he is. But that would be a lie, too, because he is not fine at all. Nobody wants a deformed orphan boy who is a little too old—at least not an employer or a foster family. But Mika understands why Rufus is so happy. For the first time in his life, he has been chosen for something. That's why he shines like the sun in his stupid corset. Somebody finally wants him, if only to use him for painful experiments.

"Congratulations," Mika says reluctantly.

Rufus looks so happy that she can't resist adding: "I hope they don't stretch you too far. I heard about a boy at Grubbens Asylum for Children who got that treatment. He was stretched so far that his arteries burst, and he died from internal bleeding. The gravedigger had to saw him into two pieces to make him fit in the casket."

"Bah!" Rufus shrugs, sending her an angry glare.

But then the corners of his mouth turn up again. No snippy comment can ruin Rufus's mood today.

When she leaves the great hall, a rough hand grabs Mika's forearm and pulls her aside.

"I gave you a task today," Amelia says in a low voice. "Maybe I wasn't clear about how important that task was.

The Department of Health has the power to determine the future of this orphanage. The building is already in bad shape, and there's talk about us having to move in a few years. But if you and I don't do our work, the children's home might well have to close, and we will end up in the street. All of us."

Amelia looks closely at Mika. Her eyes narrow when she notices her hair and her shirt.

"Where have you been?"

Mika is on the verge of telling the truth but stops herself at the last moment. Amelia already dislikes Valdemar. If Mika confesses, she may never be allowed to see him again.

"I went for a swim," she tries, and feels the grip around her arm harden.

"No dinner for you," Amelia says slowly. "The mattresses have to be ready before bedtime, understood?"

Without waiting for an answer, she drops Mika's arm and leaves the room. Mika stays behind, feeling stupid. But it's her own fault. She should have changed right away when she got home and gotten back to her work with the mattresses, instead of drawing attention to herself.

"I can help if you want me to." It's Rufus. He has squiggled out of the corset and folded it nicely into a neat package. Mika looks at him gratefully.

"No, it's my job," she says after a moment. "You go eat."

Mika puts the dirty dress back on before she returns to the yard. The cool of the evening is still far away, but a merciful shade has replaced the brutal heat of the sun. Methodically, she begins emptying the mattresses and filling them with new straw, one by one, while the smell of boiled cabbage seeps out from the kitchen, mingling with the smell of the outhouse. She thinks about what Amelia said about the children's home, that the Department of Health could close it if they wanted to. It's an unpleasant thought. But the thought of ending up in the streets is not the worst one. It's unbearable to think about how everything comes to an end. In an orphanage, nothing lasts forever. Even if the children grow up together, like siblings, sooner or later they must split up. That's why Ossian and Kristina had gotten caught up in Henrietta's scheme last spring and why Mika had ended up in jail. They can't help but dream about having a real family, a family that won't disappear at the drop of a hat. A life where nobody will come and say, *Sorry, it's over*. Henrietta had promised them that. If only it could have been true.

Axel and Margit help her carry the mattresses inside as they get done. Just before bedtime, Mika finishes the last one—her own. There is almost no straw left, only a few fistfuls at the bottom of the sack, and her mattress is as thin as a farewell letter. When Mika has rinsed herself off, she sits alone in the kitchen, eating the cabbage soup that Amelia saved for her. Her arms look like she's been fighting with a rooster; they're covered in red scratches. *Now the inspectors can come,* she thinks, and puts the bowl to her mouth to swallow the last mouthful of soup. *At least it won't be my fault if the children's home has to close.*

It's just past eleven when Mika sneaks into the dormitory. She is careful to avoid the creakiest floorboards, so as not to wake the other children. With a soft sigh she sinks down on the edge of her bed.

At night, when it's quiet, her thoughts can expand and be allowed to take up space. She tries to re-create the feeling she had during Valdemar's meeting with the Douglases. But her brain feels like it has gotten stuck and only wants to replay the same two sentences, over and over.

First, she hears Mrs. Douglas's voice saying, *My daughter can be a little messy, you see.*

Then, what Valdemar said on the way home: *If Mr. Douglas wakes up in the middle of the night with an urge, he won't have to squeeze his knees together all the way down to the courtyard.*

These sentences don't have much to do with each other. But Mika can't stop thinking about them. The words grate inside her, as if they're stuck between the two halves of her brain. Frustrated, she lies down in bed with her clothes on, prying off her boots on the footboard. She closes her eyes and imagines Beatrice's room with all her beautiful things—the desk, the bed, the bookshelves, and the heavy mirror. The picture in front of her is as still as a photograph. Only one thing moves. In the birdcage, the little finch tilts its neck on its perch and flaps its wings.

A gilded cage.

The image of Beatrice's room darkens and is replaced by another one. Even though the heat of the day lingers in the dormitory, a numbing chill spreads through Mika's body. Reflexively, she opens her eyes wide and takes a deep breath, like somebody who's had their head pushed under water. The image she just saw is of a horrible place that she once visited but never wants to return to, not even in her imagination. All of a sudden, she understands why Mrs. Douglas and Valdemar's words got stuck in her memory. Everything fits together.

Her thoughts are interrupted by a timid knocking. It comes from the window facing the street. *Hopefully, it's not somebody who wants to drop off a child,* Mika thinks instinctively. There is no room. At least not for a newborn. But people who want to drop off a child usually use the front door, not a window. Then comes another knocking, and now she recognizes the signal—three plus two.

Mika swings her legs over the side of the bed, moves quietly across the floor, and opens the curtain a little. Behind the glass, the moon shines down on a familiar figure, red wisps of hair framing a pale face, sharp cheekbones, and intense eyes. Mika quickly unlatches the window and opens it.

"Hi, Tekla," she whispers.

Something is wrong. Tekla is usually happy or angry. Usually angry. But now she actually looks scared.

"What's going—"

"You still hang out with that cop?" Tekla interrupts in a low voice.

"Valdemar?" Mika nods. "Sometimes."

Tekla looks over her own shoulder, as if worried that somebody might be listening in on their conversation.

"Come with me. I have something to show you."

If it had been anybody but Tekla, Mika might have hesitated. Now she gets her boots and throws them out the window. Then she pulls herself up on the windowsill, throws a last glance at the sleeping children, and jumps down onto the street.

CHAPTER 4

The summer night is mild and dark and smells like dew and pee. The streets are deserted except for a few unsteady night ramblers who have not yet found their way home from the bar. Mika thinks she recognizes one of the regulars from the Chapel and turns away so she won't be seen.

"Hurry up," Tekla urges impatiently, pulling at Mika's shirtsleeve.

"What are we doing?" Mika asks and takes a few quick steps to catch up.

Tekla doesn't answer. She peers nervously out across the Brunnsgatan intersection, like an animal that accidentally wandered into the city.

"It's best if nobody sees us tonight," she says.

Mika doesn't ask anything. She will find out what's going on in due course.

"I saw Valdemar yesterday," she says. "He wants to talk to you."

"He does? Why?"

"He said the police know what kind of explosive was used at the jail."

This does not seem to bother Tekla. She looks rather confused. "And?"

"The police know that it comes from one of Nobel's factories," Mika continues. "They believe it can be traced."

Tekla shrugs.

"All explosives come from Vinterviken," she says. "And we had to use the gelignite because it's easier to get the quantity right. Nellie knows exactly how much is needed to move a few rocks in a cell wall. If we had used dynamite, little pieces of you would have been scattered all over Stadsholmen Island."

Her eyes are cold when she looks at Mika.

"I don't need the concern of a cop. You can tell him that if his colleagues come after us, it will be worse for them."

Now Mika regrets having said anything. Tekla has never been afraid of the police. And if she feels threatened, anything might happen.

"Almost all the Girls are working legally these days," Tekla adds, sounding surprised herself. "The entire area of Ladugårdslandet is being built up, so we carry bricks for the stonemasons. Well, not Doris, of course, but the rest of us." Mika knows that Doris isn't part of Tekla's regular crew; she works for herself, on things they're probably all better off not knowing about.

They pass the deserted Ladugårdslandstorg Square and continue on to Sibyllegatan. The dark silhouettes of buildings, either about to be torn down or built, are everywhere. When they get close to Norra Humlegårdsgatan, Tekla stops. She pulls Mika aside, next to a collapsed shop building.

"That's where I work now," she says and points. "We have to wait for the night watchman to be done here. The same old man is in charge of all the construction jobs on the block. It takes him at least half an hour to make his rounds if he's sober, and he probably isn't."

At the building site, a flame bounces slowly across a foundation and in through the skeleton-like wooden framework on the next building site. Mika glances at Tekla. In the moonlight, her pale face looks almost ghostly.

"In order to build new, the old must be removed," Tekla whispers, without taking her eyes off the night watchman. "And when you dig in the city, you run into all kinds of things. Ruins from old chimneys, tools, cups, and plates—signs of everybody who once lived in that place. The streets we walk on were laid down on top of hundreds of years of old junk."

"What happens to the stuff that's found?" Mika asks.

"Usually nothing. It's hauled away because the building master doesn't want the work to be delayed."

As soon as the night watchman is out of sight, Tekla takes out a hurricane lamp from her bag. She lights the wick with a match and turns the flickering flame down until it's nothing but a glowing line. "Come."

Crouched, they cross the street and sneak through the wooden fence that surrounds the building site. Half of the foundation has been cleared and is ready to be paved with stones; the other half is still uneven and full of potholes. The light from the lantern is weak and Mika stumbles several times. At the north end of the lot, she sees a large shadow on the ground. When they get closer, Mika realizes that what she sees is actually a deep hole. Without a word, Tekla sits down on her butt and slides into the hole. She gestures for Mika to follow.

The fall is no more than a few feet, but since it's impossible to judge the distance, the landing is very hard. Immediately, the temperature falls and the air feels cooler. Mika's heart beats uncontrollably in her chest. She's rarely afraid in the company of Tekla, but why are they here, in a hole in the ground in Ladugårdslandet, in the middle of the night? Tekla turns up the flame and holds the lamp in front of her. At first, all that's visible is a flat wall. But as Mika's eyes get used to the light, she begins to discern some details. Buried in layers of dirt and rock are stripes and bumps, lighter than their surroundings. Broken stumps stick out from the wall like thin tree roots. Then Mika's stomach turns inside out. Because the stumps are not tree roots. They are tiny skeletons. Layer on top of layer of ribs as thin as paper, and four-inch-long femurs. Mika instinctively wants to climb back up, but when Tekla swings her lantern, she sees that there are skeletons all around the pit.

"We discovered it today," Tekla whispers, her teeth clenched. "When he learned about this, the building boss closed the site and we were sent home. I don't know what will happen."

"Was there a cemetery here?" Mika stammers.

Tekla shakes her head. "The city is full of old cemeteries and burial sites. In some places you can hardly lift a clump of grass without finding a skull. But this . . ."

She pauses, searching for words.

"This is something entirely different. The hole has been filled up little by little. And the bones are all the same size."

Suddenly, a flickering light appears above them and a man calls in a rough voice, "Who's there?"

In one swift movement, Tekla kills the flame and pushes Mika farther down into the hole. "Lie still and be quiet," she commands.

Mika can only obey; her legs fold by themselves. Tekla sticks her fingers inside her collar and pulls up a piece of fabric in front of her face, until only her eyes are visible. Then she flings herself out of the pit. A surprised yelp comes from above, followed by a few punches and low moans. Mika stays with her back against the rough bedrock. All around her, bones stick out from the walls, and high above, a wide, starlit night sky spreads out.

It's a grave, Mika thinks. *And I am in it.*

From above, she hears a muffled thump, like the sound of a body falling to the ground. Then it's quiet. After a few seconds that seem to last forever, the silence is broken by heavy breathing, and a black outline appears at the edge of the hole. Mika doesn't dare turn her head to see who it is. Instead, she tries to lie as still as she can so she won't be noticed.

"Did you fall asleep?" the outline hisses. "Get up here!"

Relieved, Mika stands and grabs the hand that is held out for her. When she is out of the hole, she notices that Tekla has blood on her face. The night watchman is nowhere to be seen.

"Now you've seen it," Tekla says quietly. "Do what you want, but keep me and the Girls out of it. Got it?"

It's not a question. Quiet as a shadow, Tekla disappears through the hole in the wooden fence, and out in the street. One last time, Mika looks at the dark hole in the foundation, then hurries out behind her.

CHAPTER 5

"Down, stupid cat!"

Valdemar shoves Lucifer down from the kitchen table. In front of him is a newspaper and a pile of old tobacco from his pipe. Valdemar stares at the little pile, as if it's trying to tell him something. He is still holding the unlit pipe in his hand, his fingers gripping the shaft.

"Children, you say?" he repeats skeptically.

Mika nods.

"Babies, I think. *Many.*"

Her hands shake a little when she lifts her mug and takes a mouthful of the bitter tea. Not because she is afraid. But when she had returned to the children's home after her night outing, climbed back in through the window, and lay down in her bed, she had been unable to sleep. As soon as she closed her eyes, she was back in that hole in the ground, with the skeletons.

Lucifer jumps up in Mika's lap. Demonstratively, he lies with his back to Valdemar and allows himself to be petted.

"All of Ladugårdslandet is practically a burial site," Valdemar points out. "Especially east of Sperlingens Backe Hill. The old paupers' cemetery used to be there, until around the time when you were born. They also buried the victims of the plague and cholera there. I doubt that they excavated very carefully before the first houses were built."

Mika shakes her head.

"I've seen old skeletal parts before," she says, frustrated. "This was something else."

"Of course, I believe you," Valdemar continues. "But I need to see it with my own eyes. Then my bosses will decide if there's enough evidence to start an investigation."

Mika spits a tea leaf into her mug and glares at him. "But there's enough evidence to look for a single runaway rich man's daughter?"

Valdemar's face is neutral when he stuffs his pipe with fresh tobacco and reaches for the matchbox. He takes a few deep breaths to get the leaves to catch, then blows the smoke toward the ceiling.

"If it were up to me, many things would be handled differently," he says eventually. "But the children you saw are dead. Beatrice Douglas is still alive—hopefully."

Mika sighs sadly. "I know. Have you learned anything?"

"I talked to the two friends, whose names I got from the Douglases," Valdemar replies. "Tora Fagerström and Hedvig von Denckert. Both are in Beatrice's class at the Wallinska School."

"What did they say?"

"What I expected. Neither of them was in the King's Garden the day Beatrice disappeared. And they had not heard that she was unhappy at home or felt threatened in any way."

"Were the girls' parents there during the conversation?" Mika asks.

Valdemar nods. "Unfortunately. Perhaps the girls would have talked more if they had not been there. But the parents insisted."

There is a rustling sound from under the kitchen bench, and Mika feels Lucifer stiffen. A moment later, he relaxes and starts purring again.

"Lazy cat," Mika says softly.

Valdemar gives her a pointed look. "Spit it out," he says, banging the shaft of his pipe on the tabletop.

"What do you mean?"

"I know that face. You have an idea."

The memory of the dark place flickers in Mika's consciousness and she shivers. "Maybe."

Valdemar's eyes light up. He hooks the pipe in the corner of his mouth and leans across the table. "Let's hear it."

"How would you describe Beatrice's room if you could use only one word?"

"Orderly," Valdemar says without having to think about it.

Mika nods. "I agree," she says. "It was clean, not a speck of dust or spot of ink anywhere. All the paper and pens were organized into perfect piles. And yet Mrs. Douglas said that her daughter was messy. And what kind of things were in the room?"

"A bed, a desk, a chair, a mirror, a birdcage, a washbasin, and a potty," Valdemar replies.

"Mrs. Douglas said that her daughter was used to a certain level of comfort," Mika says. "For example, the family has a water closet. So why did Beatrice Douglas have a potty under her bed?"

Valdemar shrugs. "A water closet makes a sound when you flush it," he says. "Maybe Beatrice used a potty at night, to not wake the family."

"Maybe," Mika admits. She pauses, stroking Lucifer's back. "Do you remember the death row cells at Långholmen Prison?"

Valdemar looks surprised at first; then he makes a face, as if he would rather forget. "What do they have to do with anything?"

"What was in the cell where John Lind sat?" Mika asks.

Valdemar sighs, then closes his eyes and focuses. "A bed, a desk, a chair, a washbasin, and . . ." A dark wave moves across his face and he opens his eyes. ". . . a potty."

Mika leans forward and puts her elbows on the tabletop. "Mr. Douglas turned the key before he opened the door to Beatrice's room. If I was a rich man's fourteen-year-old daughter with my own room, the key would sit—"

"On the inside," Valdemar finishes her sentence.

The kitchen turns quiet. The only sound is Lucifer's purring.

"You believe that they kept her locked up," Valdemar concludes.

Mika leans back in her chair. "Something wasn't right. Like I said, I believe that the Douglases told the truth. Their daughter really has disappeared. And they really do want you to find her. But I bet they didn't tell the whole truth. The Douglas family is well known and has a reputation to keep up; turning to the police is probably a last resort for them. That's why I don't believe that Beatrice disappeared last Friday. I'm guessing that she has been gone for much longer, at least a few weeks. What we saw was a rehearsed play, where only the most necessary information was revealed. The potty, the lock, and the finch made me think of something; I realized yesterday that it was a prison."

Valdemar knits his eyebrows. "Let's say the family kept Beatrice locked up. How did she manage to flee?"

"This is just a guess," Mika says. "But under the windows on the third floor, a platform runs along the entire length of the house. Between each block of stone on the wall, there is an indentation just deep enough to get a toe or a fingertip in. You don't need to be an acrobat to jump out the window and climb down to the street."

She notices Valdemar's surprised look and adds, "That's how I would have done it."

"I believe you," Valdemar says with a crooked smile. "Did you notice anything else?"

"I'm not sure, but I believe somebody was in Beatrice's room when we got there."

"Who would that be?" Valdemar objects.

"Did you notice that the teddy bear didn't seem to fit with the other items in the room? It looked like it had been played with very recently. The indentation on the bed was still warm, as if somebody had been sitting on the bedspread right before we came in."

"A younger sibling, maybe," Valdemar says.

Mika nods. "Maybe the sibling heard noises from the hallway and hid. We should talk to him or her."

"If she has a sibling, I agree it would be prudent to talk to them," Valdemar says. "But Mr. and Mrs. Douglas will never let us."

Mika balances on the back legs of her chair. "Do we have to ask permission?"

"Maybe not. But I am absolutely certain that if the Douglases find out that I went behind their back, they would contact my superiors and get me replaced."

Valdemar takes a drag on his pipe and the smoke cloud rises to the ceiling. Lucifer glares at him in disgust, as if he has done something extraordinarily improper. "Other than that, there isn't much we can be sure of. Except that this case can now be boiled down to two questions."

He doesn't need to say it; Mika already knows: "Why would somebody lock up their own daughter? And where is Beatrice Douglas?"

CHAPTER 6

The Chapel is located on a seedy street called Luntmakargatan. It is a place for those who care much less about what is on their plate than what is in their glass. It's just past eleven o'clock and, as usual, Mika is behind the bar pouring beer. For the first time in a long time, she is not constantly tense and doesn't have to hide her face as soon as a guest walks, or falls, through the door. Now that she's no longer a suspect in the jail explosion, there is no risk that somebody will come looking for her. Policemen occasionally do come into the Chapel, but most of them avoid it, afraid that they might run into somebody they locked up.

The tap hisses when Mika fills the tankard with milky foam. She expertly removes the tap from the valve and kicks the empty barrel out of the way. She hammers the tap into a new barrel with the same wooden mallet that the

Priest, the owner of the Chapel, uses on whoever refuses to pay their bill.

The floor in the dining room is a mess of pea soup, schnapps, and broken glass. Even though payday is still a few days away, lunch was messier than usual. A group of regulars from the snuff factory got into a scuffle with a group that made the mistake of sitting too close to the bar. The chaos didn't end until the Priest threatened to stop selling schnapps. Then most of them calmed down. But Mika knows that there is no reason to start cleaning the floor just yet. The regulars from the snuff factory have left, but the loud group is still here, and—considering their manners—there will probably be more to clean up. There are five men, the youngest around twenty; the rest are the Priest's age, around fifty. All of them have broad shoulders and look rather tough. The hands that grip the glasses have broken fingers and missing fingertips, their faces are scarred, and their gait is wobbly when they limp past the bar into the backyard to pee. Mika would guess that the men are dock workers, but the dock workers don't usually come all the way up to the Chapel. Maybe they're construction workers.

"That's enough for today, Daggen."

One of the older men stands up and grips the elbow of a younger man, trying to get him up on his feet. But the younger man stays seated, stubbornly, like the cows on

Oxtorget Square, who refuse to go home with their new owners. His nose looks like it's broken from the fight earlier, but that doesn't seem to bother him. The young man yanks his arm away from the older man's grip and raises his glass. Only half the drink ends up inside of him, the rest runs over his throat and down the front of his shirt. His tongue flies along his upper lip, smearing the blood from his earlier fight across his thin mustache.

Working at the Chapel has taught Mika a few things. She knows that people drink for different reasons. Some drink to forget. Valdemar is one of those; she saw that early on. What he's trying to forget, Mika has not dared to ask, but she has some theories. Some drink to reward themselves. Others to get rid of the anxiety that is slowly eating them from within. Some have drunk so much that they no longer have a choice; if their body doesn't get alcohol, they will shiver as if they're cold. The young man at the table next to the bar, however, drinks in a way that Mika has not seen before—fiercely, as if trying to hurt himself. Even though the Priest waters the schnapps down behind the counter, you can't just keep consuming it. Mika gathers empty glasses from the counter but doesn't take her eyes off the young man. There is a breaking point in the intoxication when even a person who seems unconscious might fly up and become violent. At that point, glasses and furniture might start flying. But the young man seems to be beyond that stage. Only the whites of his eyes are visible when two of the older men try to help him stand up.

"Come on, Daggen," one of them groans. "We'll all get paid less if you're not with us."

But it doesn't do any good. The heavy body is as floppy as a rag doll.

"Bah," the other one says finally. "Let's leave him here. The way he is, he won't be able to work anyway. It'll just be worse if he comes back."

The group gives up and leaves the young man at the table. Being late for work means less pay. No friend is worth that.

The Priest comes out from the kitchen and swears when he sees the comatose man.

"Why didn't you tell them to take their trash?"

"They could barely walk themselves," Mika objects.

The Priest sighs.

"Well, at least they paid, right?"

Mika nods. "They left a little extra for the trouble."

The Priest mutters to himself while checking the cash register. Then he gets the cleaning bucket and empties the contents over the man. The sudden flood of cold water brings no reaction. With a sigh, the Priest grabs the feet of the sleeping man and drags him off the bench. A meaty thump is heard when the back of his head bounces against the floorboards. The Priest measures the body on the floor with his eyes.

"Come and help."

Mika does as she is told. With a firm grip on each leg, they drag the man across the floor. The Priest grumbles about the unexpected work; he is not entirely sober himself, as usual. When they finally get the man out to the street, the Priest wipes his forehead and immediately turns to go back inside. Mika stays behind, unsure what to do. She has helped throw drunken guests out many times before and she doesn't like it. A carriage drives by, its wheels very close to the head of the unconscious man. Lying in the street entirely unprotected is very dangerous, and he is also on his back. If he vomits, he might choke to death. Mika tries to turn the man on his side and push him closer to the wall. But it's like trying to lift a two-hundred-pound sandbag. Mika stands with her legs apart, trying as hard as she can. Suddenly, she notices that the man's eyes are open. Before she can react, the man has grabbed her around the throat. He pulls her closer, his eyes cloudy.

"It wasn't me that did it."

His voice is mushy, as if his tongue is too thick for his mouth. There's an acrid smell of alcohol on his breath.

Mika tries to get away, but his grip is too strong. The man's face twists into a grimace, as if he's about to cry. "I didn't want to be a part of it."

He sounds scared, like a child.

"Wh-what?" Mika manages.

"So I didn't do what Nordlund told me to do," the man whimpers, fear glowing in his eyes. "I made sure they ended up in sacred soil."

A tear trickles through the downy bristles on his cheek. The grip hardens and Mika can no longer breathe. Desperately, she tries to open the fingers that are squeezing her throat.

"Please . . . let . . . me . . . go."

Then there is a loud bang, like the sound of a valve being hammered into a barrel. The man's grip loosens, and his eyes roll up under his eyelids. Mika falls backward in the mud. She takes a deep breath. Her throat stings. When she lifts her eyes, she sees the Priest, standing above her with the wooden mallet in his hand.

"What are you up to?" he asks suspiciously. "Are you stealing from our guests?"

Mika glares at the Priest.

"He's been robbed, all right," she says. "But not by me. What little he had is in your cash register."

The Priest pretends not to hear that. "You were lucky I came back. But I see that gratitude is not something that comes easily for you."

With a smug look, he puts the wooden mallet back in his belt.

"Well, now, don't sit here and rest. You have work to do; it looks like a pigsty in there."

It's early evening when Mika returns to the orphanage. The sun is still bright and, on the small patch of grass in the courtyard, Fanny sits with Nora and her son Henrik. Fanny is young, just a few years older than Mika. She has been baby Nora's wet nurse since spring. Mika buttons the top button in her shirt to hide the marks on her throat. Then she sits down in the grass.

"Look who's out here. Hello there, Nora."

Nora lights up and reaches for Mika. She touches Mika's face carefully, pulls her ears, squeezes her nose; then she buries her hands in the unwashed hair. Mika sits very still and lets herself be examined. After a day at the Chapel with hard work, hard words, and being strangled, it is as if Nora's soft hands take away the dirt. Suddenly, a lump forms in Mika's throat. She blinks away the tears so nobody will notice.

"She likes you. It's obvious," Fanny says, laughing. "She doesn't do that with anybody else."

Mika smiles. "I'm the one who received her when she was dropped off at the orphanage."

"By her mother?"

Mika shakes her head. "A boy dropped her off. Nobody knows who the mother is."

She still thinks of that freezing-cold night back in February. She remembers the fear in Måns's eyes, the boy who said that the Dark Angel was after him. According to Amelia, the Dark Angel is just an old ghost story that Mika should be careful not to pass on.

Fanny purses her lips. "It's one thing to be poor," she says. "But how anyone can just abandon their child like that, without even giving them a name, I just don't understand it."

Then Fanny realizes what she said, and her face turns red. "Sorry, I didn't mean—"

"I know," Mika interrupts. "It's okay. You can't miss what you've never had."

It's a lie, but Mika has said it many times before, both to herself and to others. Because she does wonder who her parents are, and why she was left at the children's home.

The only clue she has is her last name, Moonwind—and even that Amelia tried to keep from her. Amelia has always been one to hold tight to her secrets. Mika discovered it by chance, when she and Valdemar were searching through the orphanage archive in their hunt for the Night Raven last winter. That was Mika's first case.

"It's no excuse," Fanny says, ashamed. "But sometimes I forget that you're only twelve years old."

Mika shrugs. She forgets it herself. Sometimes she feels as old as Amelia. Fanny unbuttons her blouse and puts Nora in her lap. Nora nurses rhythmically, without taking her eyes off Mika. She is still too thin, but not like last spring. Each mouthful of milk, each ray of sunshine, each kind touch, makes her stronger.

You will survive, Mika thinks.

Then they hear the gate to the courtyard open. Axel and Lina arrive. They look happy. They're chewing on something.

"Where have you been?"

When they see Mika, the children look a little guilty. They both immediately swallow what they have in their mouths.

"Nothing," Axel croaks.

"I'm asking where you've been," Mika says. "Not what you're eating."

She notices that Lina is trying to hide something behind her back.

"What do you have there?"

Reluctantly, Lina holds out what looks like a dirty beret.

"It's a ball," she says reluctantly. "Somebody dumped it at the construction site. We got it because it was broken."

Axel elbows her.

"You're not allowed at the building site." Mika sighs. "How many times do I need to tell you?"

A new school is about to be built next to the children's home. It will be called Norra Latin, and only boys will be allowed to go there. Mika hates repeating herself. She knows that the way the children see her has changed, that they roll their eyes at her reprimands. But she has no choice. After what happened with Henrietta last spring, she pays careful attention to everything the children bring home.

"Give it to me," she says, holding out her hand.

"We didn't steal it, if that's what you think," Lina mutters.

Mika examines the ball. The lacing has come undone and the rubber bladder has been removed, but the leather exterior is intact. She goes to the corner of the yard where the old straw from the mattresses is still piled up. Meticulously, Mika fills the ball with straw, packs it as tightly as she can before folding the leather back in place.

Axel and Lina watch as she moves to the middle of the little patch of grass.

"Look, Nora."

Mika swings her leg, then kicks as hard as she can. The ball flies straight up in the air, high above the rooftops, until it is just a tiny dot in the sky. For a moment, it looks like it hangs in the air, not moving, then it turns and rushes back to the ground. Right then, the door to the orphanage opens and Amelia steps out onto the stairs, just in time for the ball to hit her on the head.

The yard turns totally quiet. Even Nora looks appalled. With a face that reveals nothing, Amelia bends over to pick up her glasses from the ground. She puts them on her nose and looks at Mika.

"You're having fun, I see," she says tersely.

"It wasn't . . . ," Mika begins, but she stops when Amelia motions for her to come closer.

"We have something to talk about, you and I."

CHAPTER 7

The door to the office slams shut. Amelia sits down at the desk and glares at Mika.

"I thought you were going to stay away from him," she says, her teeth clenched.

"From who?"

"Don't play dumb. The big oaf, of course."

It's hard for Mika not to smile. For as long as Amelia has known Valdemar, she has refused to say his name. Instead, she has used various, more or less accurate, descriptions for him, like big jerk, mangy bear, or doofus.

"He's been here asking for you," Amelia continues. "When you were at the Chapel."

Mika breathes slowly. "Really. What did he want?"

"Don't take me for an idiot," Amelia hisses. "He wanted you to help him, of course."

"And what did you say?"

The armchair creaks when Amelia leans back, crossing her arms. "I informed him that you have other work, here and at the Chapel."

Mika fights the anger bubbling up inside. She must not get angry. Then the discussion will be over.

"I don't need the Chapel," she says slowly.

"It's a job. You make money."

"I could make money here," Mika hears herself saying.

She regrets it immediately, but it's too late. The office gets as quiet as a burial chamber. What Mika says is both true and an accusation. She has never asked for money before.

"I wish things were different," Amelia says finally. "But you're still too young to be employed by the city, and I can't pay somebody who is not on the payroll. The work you do now is to prepare you. In due time, you will both have an official job here and be paid."

"And if I don't want to?" Mika replies defiantly.

Amelia looks surprised.

"Want to?" she repeats. "What does that have to do with anything? And why wouldn't you want to?"

Mika looks out the window, quiet now.

"You think you can be like him," Amelia says with joyless laughter.

Anger shoots through Mika and her face heats up.

"You think I'm stupid?" she exclaims. "Of course I know I can't."

Some dreams are very difficult to attain, like the ones most of the children at the orphanage have of ending up in a family where everybody gets food every day and nobody gets beaten. But then there are the dreams that are just plain ridiculous. Not even an adult woman gets to be a policeman. The most Mika can hope for is to get a job in one of the factories, or as a maid for a fine family.

"I know you're not stupid," Amelia says apologetically. "It's just that . . ." Her voice breaks and she takes a deep breath before continuing. "The first time you helped him . . . it was so horrible. Tracking down a murderer is not proper work for a child. And then, with Ossian and Kristina . . . I'm glad you did what you did, but you could have died."

As if Mika doesn't know this. Every time she looks in the mirror, she is reminded of how close she came to being killed. The injuries to her face have healed, but the thin scars from Henrietta's knives will be with her for as long as she lives.

"I'm good at doing dishes and pouring beer and wiping floors," Mika says. "But I'm good at other things too. That's why Valdemar wants me to help him. And it's different this time. It's about a girl who's disappeared."

Amelia nods. "He told me."

She reaches out to fold Mika's collar down and gasps when she sees the mark on her neck, now starting to turn green, like a grotesque necklace. She carefully touches the tender skin with her fingertips. Her eyes are black when she looks into Mika's.

"Did the Priest do this?"

Mika recoils and folds her collar up. "No," she replies tersely. "I went too close to a drunk man. It's okay, really."

Amelia watches her quietly. The setting sun breaks in through the window and lights up the dusty corners and the cracked walls of the office. The buckling rafters have thousands of tiny holes from woodworms that have slowly carved away at the skeleton of the building. Amelia leans forward and puts her elbows on the desk.

"If you turn over a rock that's been in the same spot for many years, you will find living creatures beneath it. Some will shy away from the light, scurry on to the next dark hole to hide in. And some will attack." She raises her eyebrows, pointedly, and adds, "Be careful the rocks you turn over."

"So, I get to help Valdemar?" Mika asks warily.

Amelia smiles sadly. "Haven't you already decided?"

CHAPTER 8

Rutger's hooves clop rhythmically on the cobblestones as he slowly pulls the carriage along Riddargatan. Mika sits next to Valdemar on the box seat, dressed in her best shirt and a pair of Rufus's clean pants. Even though she pretends to be unaware, she can both see and feel the looks of the people on the sidewalks. She knows what they're thinking. That she is a street rat, taken by the police, and they are on their way to the jail. But they can believe whatever they want. Even though her heart beats anxiously in her chest, nervous about what's about to happen, it's exciting to be out on assignment. Suddenly, they are passed by a fancy covered wagon pulled by a snorting two-horse team. The driver rings his bell, irritated, until he notices Valdemar's uniform. Then he stops immediately.

"No need to hurry, Rutger," Valdemar hisses between his teeth. "But it would be nice if we got there before sunset."

Mika laughs. "Don't rush him."

"There is no rushing Rutger," Valdemar mutters. "If he's in a bad mood, he won't even leave the stable. I'm the only one who uses him these days and, honestly, he is getting too stubborn even for me."

Mika says nothing. She knows that Valdemar would never choose any horse other than Rutger.

"Have you learned anything else about Beatrice?" she asks as they turn onto a new street.

"I talked to Evelina Fahnehjelm, headmistress of the Wallinska School," Valdemar replies. "She informed me that Beatrice has been taught at home since April."

"Why?" Mika asks, surprised.

"Apparently, one of Beatrice's lungs doesn't work at full capacity ever since she had consumption when she was four years old," Valdemar says. "It's not as serious as it sounds, but according to the headmistress, she has been taught at home on and off during her entire schooling, especially during the winter months."

"Why didn't her parents tell us about that?"

Valdemar flings his arms wide.

"You know what I've said about being careful with guesses. Maybe they had a reason for keeping that detail from us. Or maybe they felt that it wasn't important for the investigation. Regardless of which, I have decided not to ask the Douglases about it yet. But I did suggest that they put out an alert for Beatrice in the newspaper, with her picture. They would not even consider it."

Rutger trudges along Ladugårdslandstorg Square and on to Sibyllegatan. In daylight, everything looks different. Mika is suddenly uncertain. The building projects around them, in various stages of completion, are more numerous than she remembers, and confusingly similar. But then they cross Nya Kvartersgatan and she knows where she is again. On the right side, behind a wooden fence, corner posts stick up.

"There it is," Mika says, pointing.

Valdemar pulls at the reins and Rutger stops. He sets the brake and jumps down in the street.

"Is there a risk that somebody might recognize you here?" he asks.

Mika shakes her head. "Nobody saw me," she assures him.

"Well, then," Valdemar says and rearranges his hat. "Stay close to me."

There is frantic activity on the building site. The banging from the pavers' hammers echo between the nearby walls, and the brick carriers carry their mortar on quaking footbridges. Mika looks around for Tekla but doesn't see her anywhere. The building site looks like a totally different place today, not just because of the daylight. In the spot where the hole was, all that can be seen now is a neatly laid stone foundation. For a moment, Mika has the dizzying feeling that it was all a dream.

"Are you sure this is the right spot?" Valdemar asks when he sees her hesitation.

"Completely sure," Mika says with clenched teeth.

It's not just the stone foundation that gives her a peculiar feeling. Even though everybody around them is still working, she notices the men on the construction team exchanging looks. Several of them stand with their backs to Valdemar and Mika, but everybody seems acutely aware of Valdemar's presence. Finally, one of the stonemasons takes his cap off and walks up to Valdemar.

"Is the constable looking for somebody?"

"I would like to talk to the building master," Valdemar says with authority.

The stonemason disappears while the rest of the building crew stays in a semicircle around Valdemar and Mika. The sound of the hammers and the squeaking of the footbridges have stopped. Valdemar crosses his arms and balances on his heels, undisturbed.

"Where was the hole in the ground?" he hisses through the corner of his mouth, without looking at Mika.

"By the northeast corner," Mika whispers back. "It's covered now."

When the stonemason returns, he is accompanied by a man Valdemar's age.

"Henning Nordlund, building master." The man greets them in a friendly manner. "What can I help you with?"

"My name is Constable Hoff. I am with the police," Valdemar says. "I wonder when you put this foundation down?"

"We began laying it yesterday around noon and we just finished," the building master replies. "A little ahead of schedule. Is there a problem?"

"I don't know yet," Valdemar replies. "But laying a foundation for a building in less than twenty-four hours is quite the accomplishment. I assume that meant a fair amount of night work."

The building master stiffens almost imperceptibly. For a moment, his eyes sweep over Mika before they return to Valdemar.

"You will have to excuse me if I am too forward, Constable. But what does this concern?"

"I am here regarding a discovery on this site the day before yesterday," Valdemar replies. "You might know what I'm talking about."

"A *discovery*," the building master repeats slowly. "Please explain, Constable. Are we talking about gold or precious gems?"

Somebody on the building crew chuckles and Valdemar's face darkens. Mika secretly checks out the construction workers. Most of them are unknown to her, but one of the stonemasons in the back seems peculiarly familiar, a young man who looks like he was in a fight recently. His nose shines blue and his eyes are bloodshot. The realization is like a gut punch. It's the man from the Chapel, the one who was so drunk. The body memory makes the bruises around her neck sting. Suddenly, the man looks right at her. Mika stares back without looking away. But there is neither anger nor shame in the man's eyes. He doesn't recognize her.

"You will take my questions seriously," Valdemar says menacingly. "Otherwise, I can make sure this building project is stopped. Then you will have to wrench up every single stone that you have laid down."

"I'm sure you can do that," the building master says calmly. "You'll just need a written order from your supervisor to Jean Tellander, who owns this land and ordered the building project. But I'm sure you're aware of that."

For a moment, Valdemar looks a little crushed; then he recovers.

"Of course. Please tell Mr. Tellander that I will return shortly."

"You're very welcome, Constable," the building master replies.

Without further politeness, Valdemar turns on his heels and walks toward the exit. Taken aback, Mika is left standing alone in front of the staring building crew before she hurries to catch up with him.

"Was that all?" she protests. "I thought you had one of those orders, whatever it's called."

Valdemar shakes his head.

"I haven't talked to the chief of police yet. Like I told you earlier, we need to have something a little more substantial than a rumor for me to be allowed to start an investigation. And, in addition, Jean Tellander is the unofficial leader of the Master Builders' Exchange. To stop one of his building projects, we will probably need consent from the chief of police, something we'll never get."

"What is the Master Builders' Exchange?" Mika asks.

"It's actually Hotel Phoenix on Drottninggatan," Valdemar explains. "Every Wednesday, the most powerful building masters have lunch there while they do business. That's why the hotel is sometimes called the Master Builders' Exchange."

Mika walks up to Rutger. The coarse hair tickles the palm of her hand when she strokes his mane.

"I understand that you're disappointed," Valdemar says. "But right now, there's nothing more we can do."

"That's not it," Mika says absentmindedly.

She turns around and looks at Valdemar. "Nobody at the building site was surprised to see you. They knew that somebody would show up."

Valdemar nods. "That was obvious. I see that you're thinking about something. What is it?"

Mika hesitates before she answers.

"I don't know but . . . I recognized one of the stonemasons from the Chapel the other night. He was very drunk, and he slurred something about ignoring Nordlund's orders and making sure that something, or someone, ended up in sacred ground."

Valdemar strokes his beard thoughtfully.

"Coincidences are rarely as revealing as most people think," he says eventually. "And Nordlund is not an unusual last name. But the fact that the building master we just met has the same name is probably more than just chance."

"And whoever is looking for sacred ground around here doesn't need to look far," Mika adds.

They turn around at the same time and look down the street. Above the rooftops is the cupola of Hedvig Eleonora Church. Valdemar raises a bushy eyebrow and Mika nods in reply. Putting one foot on the hub of the wheel, she pushes off and swings herself up onto the box seat. The carriage rocks when Valdemar plops down next to her, disengages the brake, and cracks the reins.

"Change of plans, Rutger!"

CHAPTER 9

The gravedigger at Hedvig Eleonora cemetery glares at Valdemar suspiciously.

"*Unidentified remains?*" he repeats. "What's that supposed to mean?"

"A number of skeletons, to be more specific," Valdemar replies. "Or partial skeletons. That were left in the cemetery the night before yesterday."

The gravedigger examines Mika slowly from top to bottom. Then he puts a dirty index finger under his lip and digs out a large wad of snuff that he flicks into a bush.

"The deceased are usually delivered one by one," he says, wiping his finger on his pants. "And the flesh is usually still attached to the bones."

"I'm aware of that," Valdemar says, controlling his voice. "What I am wondering is if you have noticed anything unusual while performing your professional duties these past twenty-four hours?"

The gravedigger shakes his head.

"What's happened?" he asks, suddenly eager. "Perhaps I can be of help after all, if you tell me."

"Thank you, but that's not necessary," Valdemar says curtly.

Mika feels the gravedigger's eyes follow them as they return to the carriage.

"It was worth a shot," Valdemar says, sighing. "We don't even know if the skeletons were dug up before the foundation was laid."

"It's too close," Mika says, almost to herself.

"What do you mean?" Valdemar asks.

"Like I said, there were many skeletons. If they were all taken out of there, they would have made a huge pile. If it was me, first of all, I would not take all those bones to a burial site just a block away. And secondly, Hedvig Eleonora is right next to Ladugårdslandstorg Square, where people move around until late at night. Where is the next burial site from here?"

Valdemar thinks about it. "Sankt Jakob's Church, I think."

"Same thing there," Mika says. "Sankt Jakob's Church is squeezed in between the King's Garden and Jakobs Torg Square. What about the next one?"

A shadow moves across Valdemar's face. "Sankt Johannes."

Mika nods. "Maybe. Can we try that one?"

Valdemar makes a face, as if the suggestion bothers him.

"All right then," he says after a while. "If only for the pleasure of hanging out with the cemetery employees."

On their way through the city, Valdemar is uncharacteristically quiet. Rutger rhythmically trudges along Regeringsgatan. When they turn onto Drottninghusgränd, the first thing they see is the bell tower on top of Brunkebergsåsen Ridge, then the low, wooden church building. On the other side of a stone wall is a man, working on getting a tree stump out of the ground with a crowbar. Methodically, he pushes the crowbar into the ground, then rocks back and forth to break the stubborn roots.

"Are you the church gravedigger?" Valdemar calls out.

The man stops working and wipes some sweat from his forehead.

"I'm usually referred to as the custodian. Though practically, there is no real difference. And who are you?"

"My name is Valdemar Hoff. I'm with the police," Valdemar replies, stepping down from the carriage. "This might sound strange, but has something been left at the cemetery during the past few days or nights? A number of remains, to be exact."

The custodian shades his eyes with his hand. "What makes you ask that question?"

"Circumstances I wish I knew more about," Valdemar replies honestly.

The custodian watches them in silence. Then, with a swift movement, he thrusts the crowbar into the ground.

"Come with me."

Mika and Valdemar look at each other. Then they climb over the wall and follow the custodian. They walk across the cemetery, along the uneven rows of headstones and past the run-down church building. Even though it's a hot day, Mika feels a chill rising from below, almost as if it were seeping out from the very earth.

"I have worked here for more than twenty years," the custodian says over his shoulder. "In that amount of time, you see a lot. Nothing has surprised me for a while. But . . ."

He never finishes his sentence.

Squeezed in between two maples at the north end of the cemetery is a simple wooden shed with a wood-shingled roof.

"This is the old winter grave," the custodian explains. "In the olden days, it was used to store the deceased until the spring thaw. But since the north burial site opened, we've no longer had any use for it."

He pulls a key chain from his pocket and adds: "Until the night before last."

The old door swings open with a squeak.

"The girl should probably wait outside," the custodian says.

"I appreciate your concern," Valdemar says. "But wherever I go, the girl goes."

The custodian shrugs. "It's up to you, of course."

Despite the cracks in both ceiling and walls, the air in the tiny shed is heavy to breathe. The only light comes from the open door. When her eyes get used to the dark, Mika almost lets out a scream. The entire interior of the shed is full of skulls and skeletons, like a macabre death cabinet.

"I noticed two bags next to the gate by Norra Tullportsgatan," the custodian says quietly. "At first I thought it was trash that somebody had dropped off."

"Do you have any idea how many there are?" Valdemar asks, his teeth clenched.

"I can't tell you if we're dealing with complete skeletons, but counting the skulls, it might be forty-six."

Valdemar turns and fixes his gaze on the custodian. "Why didn't you go to the police right away?"

The custodian hesitates. "I don't mind helping in any way I can," he finally says. "But the people who did this are here in the city. The truth is, I'm afraid of them."

"How many people know that the skeletons are here?" Valdemar asks.

"Only me," the custodian replies. "The minister has been in Uppsala since Tuesday."

"Don't tell anyone," Valdemar orders. "Not even your superiors. And keep the door locked."

"Of course, Constable. But may I ask . . ."

The custodian clears his throat.

"Like I said, I don't mind helping. But if there is an investigation, I don't want my name associated with it."

After thinking about this for a moment, Valdemar nods. "You have my word. And you will not let anybody else see what we saw here today!"

The sun hurts their eyes when they exit the shed.

"I have some business to take care of," Valdemar says tersely to Mika. "Meet me at the carriage."

He walks away without waiting for an answer.

Mika snorts. *Some business!* Maybe Amelia isn't that far off in her assessment of Valdemar. Only a jerk would pee in a cemetery.

Then she hears the clang of a bell from somewhere. Farther off in the cemetery, she sees a woman in a nice dress, her hair done up on top of her head. When the woman bends down over a grave, Mika hears the sound again. As she gets closer, she sees that the dress, while probably nice at some point, is in tatters. The woman's hair is full of dirty, tangled snarls. A rope has been tied around her waist, and from the rope hang a pot and a frying pan; it is from them that the ringing comes. For a moment, Mika thinks it is Ladugårdslandet's White Lady, the ghost rumored to wander among the graves on the Hedvig Eleonora cemetery, hand in hand with a headless child.

Suddenly, the woman notices Mika, and her eyes open wide.

"What are you staring at?" she roars.

"N-nothing," Mika stammers, embarrassed at being caught.

"I am Dorotea de la Fleur," the woman hisses. "Has little miss not learned how to curtsy when she meets a lady?"

Mika is so surprised that she doesn't know what to do. Finally, she curtsies clumsily. The woman tucks a strand of hair behind her ear and cocks her head. Then, without a warning, she grabs the frying pan and raises it over her head.

"You're gonna get it, for making fun of fine folk!"

The woman comes closer and for a few long seconds, Mika is frozen to the ground. Then the paralysis is gone, and she runs toward the south exit where the carriage is parked. Halfway there, she sees Valdemar in the corner of the cemetery, standing by himself. Mika doesn't care if he's peeing, she will not be alone with this crazy woman.

"What happened?" Valdemar exclaims when she comes running. "You look like you've seen a ghost."

"I think I would rather see a ghost," Mika pants. "Somebody is chasing me. There!"

Valdemar turns and looks where Mika pointed. The woman is standing behind a tall headstone, glaring in their direction, visibly unhappy about having run into a police officer.

"Aha," Valdemar says, grinning. "It's your namesake."

Mika stares at him with a stupid look on her face. "What do you mean?"

"Ragamuffin," Valdemar explains. "You've heard of her, haven't you?"

Mika has heard the story of Ragamuffin, of course, the woman who fell in love with a nobleman, was betrayed, and lost her mind. But she has never seen her in person.

"I always thought it was just a myth."

"Partly," Valdemar agrees. "But myths don't appear out of nowhere; often there is a kernel of truth to them. Dorotea is well known by the police. She lives in a hut in the woods, up by Cederdal's iron ore mine. She drags all her belongings around with her so nobody can steal them."

Mika watches as the woman drops her mug on the ground and painstakingly bends down to pick it up, then disappears in a crouch around the corner of the church. There is something so sad about the whole situation.

She looks up at Valdemar. "I want to ask you a favor. Don't call me Ragamuffin again, please."

Then she notices that Valdemar is standing by a grave. A simple flat stone with nothing engraved on it.

"What are you doing?" Mika asks.

"I thought I'd visit since we're here," Valdemar explains. "I haven't been here in a long time."

He pauses before he adds, "My boy is here."

Mika feels a knot inside. Valdemar has mentioned a wife before, but never a son. So, it was this boy's shirt that she got last spring. The memory makes her feel a little ashamed.

"I was married back then and lived by Roslagstull," Valdemar continues. "We wanted a child, Karin and I, but it took a while. Finally, the boy arrived."

"What was his name?" Mika asks gently.

Valdemar is quiet for a while. Then he takes a deep breath and says, "Silas." He gives Mika a weak smile. "I don't think I've said his name out loud for five years."

Tall, sun-bleached grass grows like a collar around the stone. Valdemar crouches down and starts pulling the weeds up by their roots.

"One day, he didn't come home. We asked around among his friends, but nobody knew what had happened. Three days later, we found a note stuck under the door, telling us to search near the cliffs by southeast Kungsholmen Island. There had been an accident. Silas had been climbing the cliffs with a newfound friend but had slipped and lost his foothold. Apparently, he died immediately. His friend had heard that I was a police officer, and he didn't want me to know who he was. He feared ending up in a correctional facility for children."

Valdemar slaps the dirt from the roots of the grass before he throws it in among the trees.

"He only got to live for ten years. Now he's been dead much longer than that. It gets more and more difficult to remember his voice, or what he looked like. But sometimes I feel the weight of him in my lap, or his hand in mine. I think of it as little hatches that open, showing me the last glimpses of the person I was before I became"—he throws his arms in the air, sadly—"like this."

Valdemar stands up with effort. "After Silas's death, I was so angry. I was a bad husband, a bad police officer, a bad human being. I hurt people. The anger is still there inside of me. I fight it every day."

The scars on his knuckles turn white when Valdemar turns his hands into fists.

"It's difficult to explain, but there's a pressure that threatens to blow my skull open. Sometimes I just want to . . ."

"Drink until those thoughts go away," Mika adds. "But when the alcohol leaves the body, it feels even worse than it did before."

Valdemar turns to her, surprised. "Yes."

"I know," Mika says. "I meet men almost every day who are looking for ways to get rid of the pressure in their heads. That's how I got this."

She pulls her collar down and shows him the marks on her neck. Valdemar opens his mouth to say something, but Mika beats him to it. "I know you're not like them. But the world is divided between those who allow themselves to be controlled by their anger, and those who need to be careful. That's why we're here today. You know what I mean?"

Valdemar nods, his teeth clenched.

"I'll try to find out who Jean Tellander bought the land from," he says. "But what we've discovered today is a part of something bigger, something I can't wrap my mind around. And we still need to focus on finding Beatrice. Any ideas?"

"Not yet," Mika lies.

Because she knows that if Valdemar knew what she is about to do, he would never allow it.

CHAPTER 10

"Is it true?" Rufus whispers, amazed.

"Is what true?" Mika asks.

"That you hit Amelia in the head with a ball, of course!"

Mika sighs tiredly.

"What did Axel and Lina tell you? It's not like I *aimed* at her. It just happened—by mistake."

Rufus leans against the wall, making a groaning sound.

"Still, I would have given anything to see it. Lina said her glasses went flying."

Then he realizes that there is something unusual about the way Mika looks. Instead of her usual clothes, she is wearing a long dress and an ironed apron.

"Why are you wearing that awful costume?" Rufus asks. "I thought the Department of Health had already been here."

"I have something important to do," Mika replies. "Can you please take my shift at the Chapel? You can keep all the money. It will be a quiet day; the factory workers and the construction workers don't get paid until tomorrow."

Rufus looks tempted. He has never made any money before.

"What about the Priest?" he objects. "What'll he do when I show up instead of you?"

"Aw, he might swear and bark a little," Mika says. "But he isn't that bad, not really. He'll get over it."

She puts her hair up in a bun and secures it with a pin.

"Tell him that Constable Hoff needs my help, then he'll be nice. The Priest is afraid of Valdemar."

After a moment's hesitation, Rufus nods. "I'll do it. But if he hits me, I'm leaving."

A gray sky, heavy with rain, hangs low over Drottninggatan as Mika hurries south toward Stadsholmen Island. She meets several girls dressed like herself along the way, maids running errands for the families they work for. The Wallinska School is located on Stora Nygatan 20. Mika stops at the front door, takes a scarf from her pocket, and ties it around her hair. She looks herself over in the window and takes a deep breath. The door opens and two girls her age run outside. They don't notice Mika, who seizes the opportunity to sneak inside.

The school office is located beyond a large open space. A gray-haired woman in an immaculate dress sits at a desk next to a younger woman in her twenties.

"May I help you?" the older woman asks when she sees Mika.

"I work for the Denckert family," Mika replies and lowers her eyes. "Mister sent me here today to bring a message for Miss Hedvig."

"Oh dear," the woman exclaims. "I hope it's nothing serious."

When Mika doesn't reply, the woman purses her lips and turns to the younger woman.

"Go get Hedvig. She is in history, Rosenqvist's class."

"Is there a room where we can meet," Mika asks demurely. "Mister said that Miss Hedvig might get upset by this message."

The gray-haired woman makes a sympathetic face. "Of course. Follow me."

She shows Mika into a small room on the other side of the open space. There is only a filing cabinet, a small table, and two chairs in the room.

"You will have privacy here. Sit down and wait and Hedvig will be here soon."

Mika sits on one of the chairs but quickly stands up at a light knock on the door. Then the door handle is pushed down. Standing outside is a serious-looking girl with freckles. And behind Hedvig von Denckert is the gray-haired woman with the curious eyes.

When she sees Mika, Hedvig knits her eyebrows.

"Who's—" she begins, but she doesn't have time to finish before Mika pulls her across the threshold and closes the door in front of the older woman.

"Don't worry," Mika says quietly. "Nothing has happened. I work for the Douglas family."

Hedvig looks skeptical. "Do you? Strange that I've never seen you before."

"I just started," Mika explains. "I'm a nanny for Beatrice's sibling."

"Valter? But what happened to—"

"He misses his sister," Mika interrupts.

Hedvig nods. "I know. Everybody misses Betty. I hope she comes home soon."

"Yeah, but I think I understand why she ran away," Mika adds. "I would have, too, if my family locked me up."

Hedvig's eyes narrow and she takes a step back toward the door. Her voice trembles when she asks, "Who are you?"

"My name is Mika, and I live in the Public Children's Home. I'm sorry I had to lie. I would not have been able to talk to you otherwise. Beatrice's parents have contacted the police, and they're trying to find her."

"I know the police are looking for her," Hedvig says. "They visited my parents."

"That was Valdemar," Mika says. "You can trust him. But we know that Beatrice is staying away of her own free will. And it's very difficult to find somebody who doesn't want to be found."

Hedvig crosses her arms and looks at Mika's worn boots that stick out beneath her dress.

"You said that you live at the Public Children's Home? So, are you . . . ?"

"An orphan?" Mika fills in. "Or do you mean poor? I am both. But sometimes things are not the way they seem. I think you know this."

For a moment, Hedvig hesitates. Then she shakes her head. "I don't know what you believe. But I can't help you."

"You already have," Mika says. "I'm sorry again for lying. Please don't say anything about this to anyone."

She walks out the door, past the gray-haired woman sitting at her desk, and then out the front door. When she walks by the window, she sees Hedvig von Denckert still standing in the room, a puzzled look on her face.

CHAPTER 11

Slowly, dusk falls over Blasieholmstorg Square. The only person in sight is a lone lamplighter limping along the sidewalk. He stops in front of the door to the Douglas house, reaches with his pole toward the streetlight, and pulls the chain that opens the gas tap. Warm light floats out over the sidewalk. The lamplighter pulls a flask from his coat for a quick mouthful before he continues down toward the Stallgatan intersection.

Mika stands in the semidarkness, close to the building on the other side of the square. Her apron is rolled up in her pocket and, with her gray dress, she is practically one with the wall behind her. On the bottom floor of the Douglas family estate, shadows move back and forth behind the curtains. Mika assumes that it's the servants cleaning the dining room after supper. On the second floor, there are lights in all the windows, but the third floor, where the bedrooms are, is entirely dark. After about half an hour, the light comes on in the second window from the left. Mika feels her heart leap in her chest. It is Beatrice's room.

Mika crosses the square slowly, so as not to draw attention to herself. By the Douglas house, she makes sure that the coast is clear; then she lodges her foot in the small indentation between the rocks and pulls herself up. She is in a hurry; if somebody sees her, they'll think she's a thief. But climbing turns out to be more difficult than she expected. Mika swears under her breath about the stupid dress. When she reaches the second floor, she hears a rustling sound and the window closest to her opens slightly. Mika is left hanging on the facade like a bat, not daring to move. A thin wisp of cigar smoke trails out through the gap in the window. Mika hardly dares to breathe. She realizes that Mr. Douglas is just feet away. If he takes one step closer, he will discover her. Just when her legs begin to shake from exertion, the window closes, and Mika can keep climbing. Her fingertips ache when she finally heaves herself up onto the narrow ledge below the third-floor windows. She pauses to catch her breath for a few seconds before she starts crawling toward the window with the light on.

A boy is sitting at the desk in Beatrice's room. He looks like he is eight or nine years old. He has stuck a finger through the bars of the birdcage and smiles when the little finch bites his fingertip. Mika tries to knock on the windowpane as gently as she can, but the boy still startles. There is fear in his eyes when he rises from his chair and backs away from the window. He takes a breath, as if to get ready to call somebody, but Mika quickly puts a finger to her lips. She leans forward and breathes on the window to create fog. Then she writes, backward, with her fingertip in the condensation: RETLAV.

The boy closes his mouth. With a guarded look, he nears the window.

"Hello, Valter," Mika says when the window opens.

"How do you know my name?" the boy asks.

"Hedvig told me. My name is Mika."

Valter nods, his face serious. "I know Hedvig. Why didn't you come through the door?"

"I need to talk to your sister about something important," Mika replies. "This is her room, isn't it?"

"She's not here," Valter says immediately.

"Do you know when she'll be back?" Mika asks.

Valter shakes his head. "She won't say. She doesn't want to do what they tell her. Did you climb all the way up here?"

He looks impressed in spite of himself.

"Who says that Beatrice should do something that she doesn't want to do? Your parents?"

Valter closes his lips tightly and shakes his head. "Promised not to say."

"Good. It's important to keep your promises," Mika says. "You're a good brother. But it sounds like you can talk to your sister, even though you can't see her."

Valter is trying hard to stay silent. But then a tiny smile appears in the corner of his mouth. "The bird that can't fly whispers to me in the night when the lights are out."

Suddenly, they hear a voice in the distance. Valter turns and looks at the door.

"My mother is calling me. I'd better go."

"You seem very good at keeping secrets," Mika says quickly. "Can you promise me not to tell your parents that you talked to me? They might be angry because I didn't use the door."

Valter nods. "I promise. Careful so you don't fall down."

Then he closes the window.

Mika stays close to the buildings as she hurries home in the dark. Neither Hedvig nor Valter seem particularly concerned about Beatrice being on the run. Mika would really like to know why. But she has a feeling that neither of them will reveal more than they already have.

It's almost ten thirty when Mika returns to the children's home. As she heads for the front door, she feels somebody watching her. On the other side of the street is the outline of a dark figure, dressed in a hooded coat. Even though the late summer night is warm, Mika feels goose bumps on her arms. At first, she doesn't understand why, but then she remembers something. She is suddenly reminded of that freezing-cold night last winter when Nora was dropped off at the children's home. That same night, Mika thought she saw somebody on the other side of the street, in the exact same spot where she now sees the outline of a person.

Mika takes a deep breath and tries to steady her voice. "Hello."

The person slowly lifts her head. In the streetlight, Mika sees a woman in her twenties with tangled hair and dark circles around her eyes. Even though Mika has never seen the woman before, she feels strangely familiar.

"Are you looking for somebody?"

There is no expression on the woman's face when she looks at Mika. Without saying a word, she shakes her head, then turns around and walks south on Drottninggatan. Mika stays in the doorway until the woman is out of sight. Then she hurries inside and closes the door behind her. She checks several times to make sure the door is locked.

CHAPTER 12

"You did what?"

Valdemar stares at Mika.

"Didn't I go out of my way to tell you that the Douglases would get me fired if they suspected that I went behind their backs?"

"*You* haven't done anything," Mika objects. "And you can't keep track of me all the time."

"You're right about that," Valdemar mutters. "But I would be grateful if you would consult me before coming up with these crazy ideas."

Valdemar tries hard to look stern, but in the end his curiosity wins out and he leans across the table. "Well, did you learn anything?"

"Not much," Mika replies. "But I think Beatrice is still in town. And I believe that her brother, Valter, is in touch with her. He said something about a bird that can't fly that whispers in the night when the lights are out."

Valdemar scratches his beard. "I don't know much about fowl, but that caged bird they have doesn't say anything intelligible, regardless of the time of day. And what lights do you think he means?"

"Maybe the lamp in his room," Mika suggests. "Or the streetlights? There is a streetlight right outside the front door of the Douglas house. When do they do the half rounds on Blasieholmen Island?"

Valdemar shrugs. "Not before midnight, I should think. It's a nice part of the city."

They sit in silence for a while, thinking, but can't figure it out.

"Did you learn anything about the lot on Sibyllegatan?" Mika asks eventually.

Valdemar takes out his notebook and flips through it until the stump of his long finger reaches the right page. He groans, disgruntled about his own handwriting, as if somebody else had written these notes.

"Jean Tellander bought the property at the end of last year from a certain Mauritz Vallin, who is also a well-known property owner. But Mauritz Vallin is almost ninety years old, and the business is run by his descendants. The purchase agreement contains a legal clause about the seller not being responsible for undisclosed problems."

"Clause?" Mika says. "What does that mean?"

"It's a contract thing. It means that the seller cannot be held responsible, even if the buyer learns about some problem with the property later. Since the house was practically collapsing, it doesn't seem too strange for the contract to include a clause like this."

"Does the contract include the land that the property is built on?" Mika asks.

Valdemar nods. "But we have no proof that the seller knew about the skeletons. And we have no proof that Jean Tellander knew about them when he bought the property."

His eyebrows are knit when he knocks the shaft of his pipe against the table. "All we know is that forty-six unidentified child skeletons lie in a winter grave in Norrmalm. We don't know who they were, or what happened to them; but if the same person is behind all the deaths, we're talking about the worst murder case in the history of this city."

Valdemar balances on the back legs of his chair, deep in thought. Then he speaks again.

"This may sound like a strange question—but have you been to my apartment?"

"You mean since the day before yesterday?" Mika asks.

"It's probably just my imagination," Valdemar says, combing his fingers through his hair. "But I've had the feeling of somebody watching me for a few days now. And when I got home yesterday, the front door was unlocked." He shrugs. "I might just have forgotten to lock it. Have you noticed anything?"

Mika is about to shake her head when something occurs to her.

"Yes, maybe," she says. "Last night a woman stood outside the children's home. There was nothing threatening about her, but it felt strange."

"Did she say anything?" Valdemar asks.

Mika shakes her head. "She just stood there, watching, as if she was waiting for somebody. When I tried to talk to her, she took off."

Outside the window, a man crosses the yard. Valdemar's jaw tightens as he follows the man with his eyes. "I sometimes think of this city as a poisoned lake bottom. If you stir the sand at the bottom, the poison rises."

The man in the yard disappears through the gate and Valdemar turns to Mika again.

"I don't know why," he says thoughtfully. "But I have a feeling that we have stirred up something that has been untouched for many years. And now it is on its way up to the surface."

CHAPTER 13

Amelia reads the letter from the Department of Health with great concentration. Then she puts her glasses down on the desk with a sigh of relief.

"We're fine for now. The inspectors mention that the building is in bad shape, but we already knew this. The newborns have colds far into the spring; winters are too difficult for them. There is some talk that we will have to move."

"Move where?" Mika asks.

"The city authorities are discussing various options," Amelia replies. "The children's home has been in this building since the 1600s. We can't live here forever. Sooner or later the roof will collapse."

She smiles encouragingly at Mika.

"But that is not something that you or I can do anything about. Our job is to keep things going, like we always do."

With effort, Amelia stands up from her chair and adds, "It's getting darker earlier in the evenings now; autumn is coming. It's probably time for you to get the lamps down from the attic."

In autumn and winter, the orphanage keeps kerosene lanterns in all the rooms. During spring and summer, most of the lanterns are stored in the attic. Mika walks up the narrow stairs and opens the hatch to the attic. She carefully sticks her head through the hole and looks around. Normally, it doesn't bother her to go up in the attic. But it is August, and the bat babies are getting ready to fly. Mika moves across the squeaky floorboards as quietly as she can. From above her head comes the rustling and chirping of hundreds of creatures moving like waves between the ceiling and the outer roof. Here and there, dead pups have fallen to the floor. The tiny bodies are black like chunks of coal, the skin between their wings so thin you can almost see through it.

On a shelf by the small gable window is the children's home's supply of kerosene lanterns. Mika takes as many as she can, four in each hand, and hurries back to the hatch. Then she notices something stuck in the small space behind the chimney. Curiosity gets the best of her, and she puts the lanterns down. She sticks her hand in the small gap until she touches the item with her fingertips. Carefully, she pulls out something that resembles a large floppy balloon. Puzzled, Mika examines the strange thing. *What is it?* On one end is a mouthpiece. Mika blows into it and the balloon fills with air. After a few breaths, she realizes that she is holding the rubber insert from a soccer ball—the piece missing from Axel and Lina's ball, the one they said was broken. Mika stands there for a while, staring at the globe in her hand. Then she is awakened from her reveries by the chirping sound from the ceiling. Quickly, Mika squeezes the air from the rubber insert and puts it in her pocket. She picks up the lanterns and heads for the stairs.

When Mika comes downstairs, Rufus is standing in the entryway. He is wearing a clean shirt, struggling with the buttons on his sleeves.

"Are you going for your treatment today?" Mika asks.

"They're coming to pick me up anytime." Rufus laughs and shakes his head. "Can you imagine me traveling alone in a carriage, like a nobleman."

"Don't get used to it," Mika says. "Soon everything will be back to normal. Then not even the waste collector will give you a ride."

"I hope so," Rufus says with a pale smile. "Then my back will be all better."

Mika has the urge to stroke his back, but she resists. "Does it hurt a lot?" she asks.

Rufus nods.

"Yes, but I try to think about something else. That helps a little. Tell me if you want me to cover more of your shifts at the Chapel, by the way."

"You liked it?" Mika says.

"Not exactly," Rufus replies. "At first, the Priest was angry. Asked why you sent a cripple instead of coming yourself. But then he let me work anyway, and it went well. At least well enough that I got paid."

"Put the money in a safe place that only you know of," Mika cautions. "Or it'll disappear."

Rufus looks a little embarrassed. "I already bought something."

He puts his hand in his pocket and pulls out a tiny figurine. An ocarina.

"It was Lina's," Rufus explains. "She got it from one of the construction workers by the new school."

"I told her not to—"

"Calm down." Rufus sighs. He can tell that Mika is getting irritated. "I've talked to the construction workers too. They're nice. Some of them grew up in an orphanage. They know what it's like for us."

"Don't tell me to calm down," Mika hisses.

She holds her hand out in a way that leaves no room for an argument. "Let me see it."

"I bought it with my own money," Rufus says.

"Yes, you told me."

Mika takes the tiny bird ocarina. The sides are decorated with a pattern that looks like feathers. There is a beak, and the eyes are sculpted with fine details. She puts her mouth to the bird's behind and blows. A low tone comes from a hole by the beak.

"Be careful," Rufus scolds her. "It's fragile."

Mika carefully runs her finger along the textured wings. The burnt clay feels rough against her fingertip, almost like stone. She suddenly remembers something from the house on Blasieholmstorg Square—the gray building facade and the front door with its thick glass panes.

"The bird that can't fly whispers to me in the night when the lights are out," she mumbles.

"Give it back." Rufus grabs the ocarina from Mika and glares at her. "Maybe you should come to the hospital with me," he snorts. "You need help."

CHAPTER 14

School is out for the day. A thunderous roar comes from the staircase when the horde of big children rushes down. Mika grabs Lina's arm and pulls her aside.

"Can I talk to you?"

Mika waits until the others have disappeared into the dining room. Then she takes the rubber insert from her pocket. "I found this in the attic."

Lina shrugs dismissively. "What's that got to do with me?"

"I just wanted to tell you that I know what you and Axel are up to," Mika says quietly. "And I told Constable Hoff about it. He's coming to talk to you this afternoon."

Lina's face flushes with color and her eyes flutter. "You'd never," she gasps.

"Wouldn't I?" Mika says. "We'll see."

Calmly, she folds the rubber insert and puts it back in her pocket. Then she turns and walks toward the dining room. She is halfway through the hallway before she hears Lina's voice.

"Wait!"

Lina walks fast to catch up with her.

"It's true that we got the ball from the construction workers," she whispers. "Somebody had kicked it in under the fence and the workers wanted to be nice. But it was Axel's idea to switch out the rubber insert."

"Switch it out for what?"

Mika waits in silence, arms crossed. Finally, Lina sighs.

"You know what it's like when orphans come into a store. Even when we haven't taken anything, they follow us around and check our pockets. But nobody thinks to check a soccer ball. We took the rubber insert out and put in some other things. Chocolate, mostly."

"So, if everybody believes that children from the orphanage steal, we might as well do it," Mika says. "Is that what you mean?"

Lina looks away and remains quiet, defiant.

"How can you do that when you know what happens to orphans who steal?" Mika hisses. "You could end up in jail!"

Lina's eyes tear up with shame. "You never do anything you're not supposed to?" she asks quietly. "Take something without asking?"

"I almost did last winter," Mika says honestly. "I could have stolen then, so we would have had more to eat. But I went to jail once, and I know what it's like to be locked up. I wouldn't risk it for a piece of chocolate, or an ocarina."

Lina leans her head against the wall, moaning. "Rufus... I should have figured it out. Did he tell on me?"

"You gave it away yourself," Mika replies. "All I knew was that Rufus bought an ocarina from you. You said it yourself, just now."

Lina looks crushed.

"Stealing is one thing," Mika continues. "But when you sold your stolen goods to Rufus, it made him an accessory. I feel like reporting you just to protect him."

"I thought you already had," Lina mutters.

"I haven't decided yet."

Mika puts her hand in her pocket and gives Lina the rubber insert. "Now go eat until you're full so you don't have to steal. And be sure to fix the soccer ball."

After lunch, Mika hurries south through the city. Rufus's ocarina has given her an idea. Maybe it won't lead to anything, but it's worth a try.

By Blasieholmen Island, Mika positions herself at the intersection of Arsenalsgatan. Then she waits. Down the street, a maid comes out a front door to empty a bucket of water in the gutter before she disappears back inside. When the sidewalk is empty again, Mika starts walking. On each side of the Douglas family's front door are the stone pillars with the falcon ornaments. Mika stops at the left falcon and quickly puts her hand in the mouth of the bird. Inside the open beak is an empty space. Then she does the same thing to the other falcon. Her heart jumps when her fingertips touch something hard. Hidden inside the falcon's mouth is a small shiny metal tube; it looks like a silver cigar case. Mika looks around quickly; then she unscrews the lid. Inside is a rolled-up piece of paper. With shaking hands, Mika teases the paper out. It's a letter. The handwriting is angular and childish, the paper full of inkblots, but it's legible.

> Dear Sister,
> You don't need to be afraid. I have not told anybody. Father and Marianne want you to

come home. I heard them talking. They said that the trip will be quick. Then you get to come home again. Ivar is gone. That's sad. Father says I am not allowed to talk about him. I miss you and I miss Ivar.

    Sincerely, Valter

Mika reads the letter quickly, twice. Then she puts it back in the tube and puts the tube back in the mouth of the falcon.

"Hello there, who are you?" The voice comes from above. A maid is washing a window on the second floor. "What are you doing?"

Mika hides her face with her shawl and hurries toward Arsenalsgatan. You can't hide in the square in full daylight. She doesn't dare wait for Beatrice to appear; it's too risky. And Beatrice might not even be the one who picks up the letter.

When Mika has passed Jakob's Church, she slows down. She thinks about Valter's letter. Why did he call Mrs. Douglas Marianne? And what is the trip that their parents want Beatrice to take? She also wonders who Ivar is. Maybe another brother. Or a fiancé. She wishes she could talk to Valter again.

As Mika turns onto Drottninggatan, she freezes in place. In the street, some distance away, she sees a hooded figure dressed in black. It is the strange woman from the other night. She just stands there, unmoving, staring at the orphanage.

CHAPTER 15

Mika gathers courage. Then she carefully approaches the woman, step by step, stopping far enough away that she'll be able to escape if something should happen.

"Who are you?"

The woman startles at the sound of Mika's voice.

"I'll leave," she says, frightened. "I'm just—"

"Why are you standing here, in front of the children's home?" Mika interrupts. "Who are you looking for?"

"Nobody. It's just . . ."

Then, suddenly, it seems as if the woman realizes that Mika is a child. Her shoulders drop and her whole body relaxes.

"I think my girl lives here. She was dropped off at the children's home on February twentieth."

Now it is Mika's turn to startle. She notices the woman's dark eyes, the hair that curls around her temples, the soft look around her eyes that feels so familiar.

"Nora?" she asks slowly. "Are you her mother?"

"She didn't have a name," the woman says. "You call her Nora?"

"She was baptized Nora," Mika says. "I was the one who received her when she was dropped off at the orphanage."

Before Mika can react, the woman takes a step toward her and seizes her arm. "How is she? Is she well?"

Mika raises her hands and pushes the woman away. It's easy. Despite their age difference, they are the same height, and the woman is malnourished and weak.

"I'm sorry," she says. "It's just . . . I've missed her for so long."

Mika looks at Nora's mother, distraught over the loss of her daughter, and hesitates. The rules are clear and hard: no strangers are allowed in the orphanage. But in the back of Mika's mind, Lina's words echo. *You never do anything you're not supposed to?*

At that moment, she makes a decision.

"Do you want to see her?"

Nora is in her bed in the younger children's dormitory. Fanny is sitting by the window with Henrik in her lap.

"I have some downtime," Mika says, lifting Nora up in her arms. "I'm taking her outside for a bit."

In the hallway, she speeds up and looks over her shoulder to make sure Amelia is not nearby. She sneaks out into the inner courtyard and continues to the part that's hidden by the woodshed. When the woman sees Nora, she puts her hand in front of her mouth and sobs.

"It's her, I can tell. Please, may I hold her?"

The woman weighs Nora in her arms and gently pinches the skin on her forearm, as if to measure how well fed she is.

"She looks healthy. Is she?"

Mika hesitates. Just a few months ago, Nora was close to dying. Should she tell her that, or not?

"She was weak for a while. She's better now."

The woman strokes Nora's head, twists her soft hair between her fingertips. She carefully examines her fingers, her ears, her toes, as if to store every little detail in her memory. Nora lies completely still in her arms with a serious look on her face. When the woman has been reassured that Nora is fine, she relaxes a little.

"My name is Cecilia, by the way," she says, without taking her eyes from her daughters'. "Nora is a nice name—did you come up with it?"

Mika nods. "Nora was wearing a rose band when she was dropped off," she says tentatively.

Cecilia gets a strange look on her face. "I know I'm not supposed to be here. I just want to see that she's fine. Once, before . . ."

She stops, as if afraid to finish the sentence.

"Why did you leave her?" Mika asks.

Cecilia smiles sadly. "The boy I met comes from a good family," she says. "We were not married, and I am also older than he is. His parents could not accept me, or the child. They arranged for me to go to a special place where somebody would help me have the baby. But I would not be allowed to bring the baby home."

"What kind of place was it?" Mika asks.

"We were never told. Just that a carriage would be sent for us when the time came. But my fiancé and I made plans to save Nora. We got help from a boy who worked for the family."

"You mean Måns?"

Cecilia looks frightened. "You may absolutely not mention his name to anybody. That would make him disappear. *Promise me!*"

"I promise," Mika says. "But what was going to happen to Nora? Was she going to another orphanage? Or to someone else?"

Cecilia shakes her head. "Believe me, it's better for you not to know."

"People have kept things from me my entire life," Mika says. "And I have learned that you can't protect anybody by hiding the truth."

Cecilia leans over Nora, touches the tip of her nose to her head, and inhales her smell. When she looks at Mika again, her eyes are shiny with tears, her voice barely more than a whisper.

"It's the Dark Angel."

CHAPTER 16

Mika once saw a rat in a cage. The rat was furious. It flew around, hissed, and screeched like a monster. That's how Mika feels now. Her pulse is racing and her thoughts bounce from side to side in her head like desperate caged animals, clawing at the walls to find a way out. Words and sentence fragments pop up in her brain but they don't stick.

Like what Cecilia said:

They arranged for me to go to a special place where somebody would help me have the baby. But I would not be allowed to bring the baby home.

Then Valter's note; angular letters on a piece of paper covered in inkblots:

You don't need to be afraid . . . They said that the trip will be quick. Then you get to come home again.

The note fades from her mind and is replaced by a voice. It belongs to the custodian at Johannes Cemetery:

been locked up in the Madman's Palace. What if her mother is a Ragamuffin, too—a poor, helpless thing betrayed by a nobleman and who has lost her mind? A dirty, toothless, crazy person who looks for food in the gutters, somebody who people either laugh at or are afraid of. The thought is unbearable. It grates inside of Mika.

The next thought is forbidden, but she can't stop it.
In that case, it's better if she's dead.

Mika's throat is so dry that she can barely swallow. She stands up from her bed and moves quietly to the door. In the kitchen, she takes a mug of water from the bucket on the bench. The water is tepid and tastes like tin, but she drinks it down in large gulps. On the other side of the window, the moon shines across the inner yard of the children's home. Mika feels hopeless. The only thing she has managed to do is put herself and Valdemar in danger. What should she do? Valdemar might be murdered anytime, and Beatrice Douglas is still gone. Mika dips her cup in the bucket and fills it again. While she drinks, her eyes find the soccer ball in the yard outside. The children have played with the ball every day since Lina fixed it. Mika feels something begin to stir in her mind. Like lice searching for thin skin, her thoughts take off in different directions; but they end up in the same place—the tiny indentation at the back of her neck. In her mind, Mika hears Lina's voice:

But the people who did this are here in the city.

Mika's head feels like it's about to explode. She closes her eyes and pushes her fists to her temples. Suddenly, her thoughts stop racing and everything gets calm. A cool evening wind moves through the room as she falls asleep, and Mika dreams. She sees a sparkling starry sky spread out above her. She is back in the pit on Sibyllegatan. The cold from the bare ground seeps into her back. Slowly, Mika turns and sees the skeletons buried in layers of dirt and sand. Right next to her face, a lower leg bone sticks out from the wall. Something is attached to the ankle. In the faint moonlight, she sees a narrow leather band with a pattern of red roses.

As if somebody has poured a bucket of freezing water over her, Mika opens her eyes wide and fills her lungs with air. She understands now. Amelia's lies about the Dark Angel, the case with Beatrice, the unidentified children on Sibyllegatan. They are all separate but also not.

Everything belongs together.

And it is worse than she could ever have imagined.

CHAPTER 17

Mika runs as if her life is at stake. Her heart hammers wildly in her chest as she zigzags between the carriages on Klara Västra Kyrkogata. At one intersection, she cuts so close in front of a carriage that the horse spooks and rears up. The coachman swears and tries to hit her with his whip. When Mika finally reaches Valdemar's apartment building, her lungs are screaming for oxygen, and she tastes blood in her mouth. She yanks open the door of the building and takes the stairs in four steps. On the second floor, Valdemar's door is ajar. Relief washes over Mika. He's home.

When Mika walks inside, she sees Lucifer lying like a sentry between the entryway and the room. He is usually happy to see her but today he arches his back and hisses, as if she were a stranger, before he escapes out the door and disappears down the stairs.

"Hello?" Mika calls into the apartment.

Valdemar is nowhere to be seen. *Maybe he accidentally left the door open?* Carefully, Mika steps in over the threshold. There is a peculiar smell of metal in the air. On the floor is a pool of some dark liquid. *Spilled soup,* Mika thinks. Then she notices two feet sticking out from behind the kitchen table, and the skin on her neck contracts. Valdemar is spread out flat on the floor, his hands closed around the shaft of a knife that sticks out from his chest, as if he tried to pull it out but didn't have enough strength. The dark liquid is not soup but blood.

Mika falls to her knees next to him.

"V-Valdemar," she stammers. "Are you alive?"

Valdemar's eyelids twitch and he opens his eyes. He lets go of the knife and reaches for Mika with his hand. His face contorted with pain, he pulls her toward him.

"Go . . ."

His voice gets weaker and he has to take a breath to continue. From his chest comes a horrible gurgling sound.

". . . hide."

With a slow breath out, Valdemar lets go of Mika and his hand falls to the floor. Time stops. Mika sits still, turned to stone, staring at the motionless body in front of her. Then she gets up on her feet and runs out into the stairwell. She fills her lungs with air. The sound that comes out of her throat is a wild howling. A door opens above her, and a man takes a few careful steps down the stairs.

"What happened?"

Mika's legs fold and she falls into a little pile on the floor.

"It's Valdemar!" she sobs. "He's dead."

CHAPTER 18

The voices are unfamiliar and seem to come from a place far away. Slowly, they enter Mika's deep sleep and dig their way into her consciousness.

"We thought she was his daughter," one of the voices says. "She was as stubborn as a wild dog; we could barely get her out."

"As far as I know, Hoff doesn't have any children anymore," the other one says. "This one looks more like a street rat."

A rough shaking pulls Mika out of her sleep. She opens her eyes; she is on the floor of the entryway to the hospital, her back to the wall. Above her tower two unknown men—one in a police uniform, the other in a doctor's smock.

"Constable Hoff is alive," the man in the doctor's smock says dryly. "You may leave now."

"I want to see him," Mika slurs, standing up.

"He is unconscious," the doctor says sharply. "You wouldn't even be able to see him if you were next of kin. Which you are not, if I understand correctly."

Mika glares at the doctor.

The police officer demonstratively puts his hand on the baton by his belt. "If you don't leave voluntarily, I will have to help you."

It is not far from Sabbatsberg Hospital to Drottninggatan. Mika walks as if in a fog, still exhausted from the previous night. As recently as the other night, Valdemar said he felt as if somebody was watching him. And now he is unconscious in the hospital, stabbed in the chest. Who did this to him and why? Mika knows it has to do with the skeletons. *Do what you want, but keep me and the Girls out of it*, Tekla said that night when she showed Mika the hole in the ground on Sibyllegatan. The custodian at Johannes said the same thing. The only one giving his name was Valdemar, when he visited the building site. That must be how they found him. Mika angrily wipes away her tears with her shirtsleeve. Stupid, careless Valdemar.

At the orphanage, Mika goes straight to the office. She opens the door without knocking. Amelia is sitting with her back to her, working on something in the archive cabinet. When she turns around and sees Mika, she looks both relieved and angry.

"Where have you been all night? I want to remind you—"

"You've been lying to me," Mika interrupts. Suddenly, her exhaustion from the previous night is gone. Anger makes her blood move faster and sharpens her senses.

"You have accused me of lying before," Amelia says, pursing her lips. "Are you thinking of something in particular?"

"My entire life," Mika replies. "You told me that the Dark Angel was a made-up ghost story. I know that's not true. And now somebody has tried to murder Valdemar. He is at Sabbatsberg Hospital, and I don't know if he'll survive."

The words seem to slap Amelia in the face. She sinks back in her chair and puts her hand over her mouth.

"This is what I've been afraid of," she says. "If *that guy* survives, you will never be allowed to go near him again. Or it will be your turn next time."

"His name is Valdemar," Mika says quietly. "And it's time we talk."

For a long time, Amelia sits quietly, staring empty-eyed in front of her. Then she nods, relenting.

"I know you know about the rose bands," she says. "They are a message to the orphanage. It means that the fee will be paid, and that the child will never learn about their heritage."

"Is that why I'm not allowed to know anything about my mother and my name?"

The loose skin on Amelia's cheeks twitches.

"I promise it was for your own safety," she whispers. "You must not believe anything else."

"Maybe it was safer for me not to know before," Mika says. "But that's not true anymore. The more I know now, the greater the chance that I make it."

Amelia stretches, as if to prepare herself for what she is about to say.

"In some ways, it is like a ghost story. Nobody knows the identity of the Dark Angel. Over the years, she has become more of a myth than a human. But yes, she exists in real life. She is an angel-maker. Powerful families that want to get rid of unwanted heirs send their daughters or their sons' girlfriends to the Dark Angel. After the child is born, the girls go home."

"But the children stay," Mika completes her sentence.

Amelia nods with clenched teeth. "And nobody knows what happens to them."

Trembling, Mika thinks about the hole in the ground on Sibyllegatan. How many secret graves are out there that nobody has yet discovered? Valdemar was not exaggerating when he talked about the biggest murder case in the history of the city.

"The Dark Angel was supposed to get you," Amelia continues. "But your mother managed to save you somehow and you ended up here with me."

"What happened to her?" Mika asks. "My . . . mother?"

A lone tear runs down Amelia's cheek. It's the first time Mika has seen her cry. "My dear . . ."

"Tell me!" Mika demands.

"I know that she was committed to Konradsberg . . ." Amelia takes a deep breath. "And from what I heard, she never got out."

Mika feels her legs fold and she has to sit down. Her heart is beating hard in her chest. She knows very well what Konradsberg is. It's a mental hospital on Kungsholmen Island, sometimes called "Madman's Palace."

"All I know is that your fee is paid on time, once a year," Amelia says. "I don't know if Moonwind was your mother's real last name, or who your father was. You must believe me when I say that everything has been kept confidential with your welfare in mind. Yours and that of all the roseband children."

Mika pulls away from Amelia's outstretched hand. She sits quietly for a while, then says, "I have to stop it."

Amelia smiles sadly. "The people who hire the Dark Angel are prepared to pay to get rid of a child. What do you think they would do to an orphan trying to expose them? And what if they find out who you really are, and that there are others like you—children who didn't disappear? They wouldn't want to risk those heirs coming forward, exposing them, causing trouble."

She strokes Mika's arm.

"I meant what I said. I think the only thing that can save you now is to stay away from Constable Hoff. Otherwise, you risk not only your own life, but the lives of all the roseband children. Think of Nora."

Mika doesn't reply. She will do anything to protect Nora. But the Dark Angel is still receiving children. Who will protect *them*?

Right now, Mika knows only one thing: if Valdemar dies, everything is over; then they won't be able to do anything at all.

CHAPTER 19

"It was my fat that saved me," Valdemar announces happily. "The doctor said that it protected my vital organs from the knife."

He gingerly pats his stomach, which is almost entirely wrapped in a thick bandage.

"And that I got to the hospital in time, of course," he emphasizes. "Otherwise, I would be lying under a sheet in the morgue right now. As I understand it, that's all thanks to you."

Mika doesn't know what to say. It's terrible to see Valdemar in a hospital gown with those white, bony legs sticking out, and the bloodstained bandage.

"How long do you have to stay in the hospital?" she asks.

"They can't say exactly," Valdemar replies. "The wound has been stitched up. The problem is the loss of blood. I've been stabbed before and hit in the chin, but never stuck like a pig. If I tried to stand up, I would faint."

Mika gives him a serious look. After a moment, she says, "I met Nora's mother. She said the Dark Angel is real."

Valdemar looks a little ashamed. "I know."

Mika raises her eyebrows. "You do?"

"It's the reason you and I met that first time," Valdemar says. "I read Westerberg's report from when Nora was dropped off at the orphanage. You mentioned the Dark Angel in there. I went to find you because I was curious. Then the Night Raven entered the picture and we had other things to think about."

He smiles at Mika's surprised look.

"There is no formal investigation about the Dark Angel. But the police have known of her existence for years. Everybody who tries to look into it ends up in a bad way. Many powerful people want this to stay secret."

"Like Mr. and Mrs. Douglas," Mika says.

Valdemar looks taken aback. "What are you saying?"

"I found a letter to Beatrice from her brother," Mika says. "I'm not sure, but I think she's pregnant."

"The girl is not even fifteen," Valdemar objects.

"So what?" Mika snorts. "Who do you think leaves their newborns at the orphanage? Most of them are still children themselves."

"I do know that," Valdemar agrees. "But there is a difference between how the wealthy and the poor solve their problems, as you well know."

He fondles his beard thoughtfully.

"But that would explain a few things. Like why Beatrice has not been allowed to go to school since April. And why they kept her locked up so she wouldn't run away."

"Do you think this has to do with how you ended up here?" Mika asks.

Valdemar nods, his face white. "I made a mistake on Sibyllegatan, giving my real name," he says. "If the skeletons can be connected to the Dark Angel, then my life isn't worth much. Neither is yours, come to think of it."

Mika nods. "Amelia said I should stay away from you."

"She's right," Valdemar agrees. "You and I have been in danger before, but this is something different."

He glances out in the hallway, as if to make sure that they're alone.

"What should we do then?" Mika asks, frustrated. "Give up because it's too dangerous? And let more children die?"

"First things first," Valdemar says. "If the person who tried to murder me doesn't already know that I survived, he will soon find out. And then he will come back to finish the job. I need a weapon. A gun, preferably."

Mika looks at him incredulously. "Where do you think I would get a gun?"

Valdemar gives her a weak smile. "How about a knife then. Or a very sharp fork?"

It is meant as a joke but neither of them laughs. They both know that if the murderer comes back, Valdemar doesn't have a chance.

Mika thinks about what Amelia said, about the creatures that live under rocks.

Some will shy away from the light, scurry on to the next dark hole to hide in. And some will attack.

"What day is today?" she asks.

"Wednesday, I believe," Valdemar says. "Why?"

"I have to do something. See you soon."

Mika takes off for the exit. In the hallway, she passes something that looks like a classroom. Along the walls are shelves with books and boxes with instruments. In front of one of the shelves hangs a skeleton on a stand. Mika stops. She looks around quickly; then she goes into the room, lifts the head off the skeleton, and wraps it up in her shawl. None of the staff notices her when she sneaks by the front desk, crouching, and out into the street.

CHAPTER 20

"What does this say?" Tekla asks, putting her index finger on the Hotel Phoenix menu.

"Chateaubriand," the surly maître d' replies. "It is the finest cut of beef tenderloin, served with a chanterelle mushroom and cognac stew."

"Well, then I don't want it. I'm tired of beef tenderloin," Tekla says. She bites off a dirty fingernail and spits it over her shoulder. "Do you have frog legs? I've been wanting frog legs since my last trip to Paris, you see."

"Not for lunch, I'm afraid," the maître d' replies, examining Tekla from top to bottom. "If *my lady* would excuse me, we have a certain . . . dress code."

"No excuse needed," Tekla says, patting the maître d' on his shoulder, as if to console him. "It's not easy to get a bow tie just right. You'll learn soon enough."

Mika quietly walks up to them. In her arms, she's holding Amelia's old leather briefcase.

"I have a message for Mr. Tellander," she says to the maître d' in a low voice. "It's a contract that needs his signature."

"They are seated in the Back Pocket," the maître d' replies, and waves her on without taking his eyes off Tekla.

Hotel Phoenix is the opposite of the Chapel. The guests here are dressed in suits and fine dresses. On the tables are bright-white linen tablecloths, and heavy chandeliers hang from the ceiling. Not a single person eats with their fingers or is too drunk to sit in a chair. Mika walks through the dining hall with the briefcase pressed to her chest. Farthest from the entryway is a separate room called the Back Pocket. Through thick cigar smoke, Mika can make out seven men sitting around a table full of bottles, glasses, and empty plates. The sounds of laughter and loud voices bounce against the walls in the small room. Mika waits in the doorway until one of the men discovers her.

"What can we do for you, young lady?"

Mika clears her throat. "I am looking for Jean Tellander, who is building on Sibyllegatan 24."

The members of the Master Builders' Exchange give each other an amused look, as if Mika has just said something funny. At the head of the table sits a man with a well-groomed salt-and-pepper beard and icy blue eyes. The man examines Mika, then takes a last puff on his cigar before he puts it out in a puddle of sauce on his plate and blows the smoke toward the ceiling.

"I am Jean Tellander," he says. "What is this about?"

"I would like to speak to you in private," Mika says.

A look of understanding passes between Tellander and one of the other men in the group, and the other man snaps his fingers at one of the waiters. When the waiter sees Mika, he grabs her arm roughly.

"Are you begging at the table, child?"

Just as the waiter is about to throw Mika out, she reaches into the briefcase and pulls out the item that she brought to the restaurant. The very moment she puts it down on the table, the room turns quiet. Among wineglasses and dirty plates sits the skull from Sabbatsberg Hospital.

"I have a few questions about the skeletons that were found on Sibyllegatan 24," Mika says.

The waiter starts pulling her toward the exit, but Tellander raises his hand. "Wait."

He turns to the other men. "If you would be so kind as to excuse us, gentlemen. It seems I will have to clear up a misunderstanding. It will be quick. Meanwhile, have an avec, and tell the maître d' to put it on my tab."

The members of the group look a little surprised, but they obediently follow the waiter to the bar. As soon as they are alone, Jean Tellander's eyes bore into Mika's.

"You have something to say to me?" he asks, ice in his voice.

"Valdemar is alive," Mika says. "I thought you might want to know."

"I don't know anybody named Valdemar," Jean Tellander says. "And why would I be interested in the health of this person?"

"Because if he or I die, the police will immediately be informed of the skeletons and led to where they are," Mika replies. "Then you will be accused of trying to stop the investigation of the murder of forty-six children."

"This is absurd," Tellander snorts. "There were never any skeletons on Sibyllegatan, or any of my other lots. Is this an attempt at blackmail?"

"I'm just telling you what will happen," Mika says. "I guess it's more of an information session. You don't have to worry about the court; it will probably free you. Your punishment will be different."

When Master Builder Jean Tellander leans across the table and nails Mika with his gaze, his eyes are aglow with withheld anger. "Little girl, you have no idea who I am, or what consequences your accusations will have. Go ahead and tell me what my punishment will be."

"In time, people will forget exactly what happened," Mika says. "But the rumors will keep spreading, details will be changed or added, until the story takes on a life of its own. Much like it is with the Dark Angel, if you've heard of her? The name Tellander will be forever attached to the murder of children. Your apartments will be difficult to sell. Your colleagues will pull away. You will sit here alone with your lunch."

She holds the skull in her hands for a moment, before she puts it back in the briefcase and adds, "As alone as you are now."

Jean Tellander looks over his shoulder. Then he says loudly, so they will be able to hear it in the dining room, "Like I said, I don't know what you're talking about."

He wets his lips and looks longingly at the wine bottle on the table. When he opens his mouth again, his voice is low, almost pleading, "What happened to your friend is regrettable. I hope he gets well soon."

"Thank you," Mika says. "I will tell him that from you."

She takes her briefcase and walks back through the dining room, ignoring the eyes of the rest of the members of the Master Builders' Exchange who have lined up by the bar.

Outside the restaurant, Tekla is waiting, her back against the wall.

"What have you gotten yourself into?" she says. "Those old men are not just anybody."

"Somebody tried to murder Valdemar," Mika replies. "And they might try again. This was a bluff, to buy some time."

"That balding ox of a cop?" Tekla snorts. "Who would want to murder him?"

"More people than you know," Mika says. "Valdemar and I have been investigating the skeletons that you showed me. We believe they're tied to the Dark Angel."

Tekla's eyes widen.

"Is that what this is about?" she exclaims. "You're crazy, Mika. I have warned you before, certain things should not be messed with."

Mika nods. "I know. And I don't want to get you mixed up in this, but Valdemar needs protection."

Tekla mutters to herself. "I'll see what I can do," she says eventually. "Do you need anything else? A kilo of gold? The left shoe of the queen?"

"Well, actually," Mika says carefully. "I need to talk to Doris."

Tekla's red eyebrows shoot up to her forehead. "Doris? Get in line. Half the police departments in the country are looking for her."

A police carriage comes thundering down Drottninggatan at just that moment and Tekla shrinks into the shadows. Her eyes shine like a cat's in the dark.

"Are you doing this for him?"

"I'm doing it so no more children will have to die and get thrown into a hole," Mika replies.

"That's noble of you," Tekla says sullenly. "How are you going to use all this heroism when you yourself lie there at the bottom of a pit?"

Mika glares at her. "I'm doing this with or without your help."

Tekla's bony face lights up in a menacing smile.

"Excuse me so very much, Mika Moonwind. But the heck you are."

CHAPTER 21

Sankt Johannes Cemetery is shrouded in a thin morning fog. The grass is wet with dew and from one of the linden trees above comes the song of a blackbird. Mika walks alone among the rows of headstones. Even though she was here recently, she still doesn't quite know her way. Maybe it's the fog, but everything feels larger somehow. The row of graves never ends; it goes on and on, into the gray fog. Soon, she can no longer see the church. This can't be right. Mika decides to turn around and walk toward the exit. But it looks different from the way she came. The headstones are taller here, and closer together. It almost feels like walking in a labyrinth. Suddenly, she hears a sound in the distance. It reminds her of a windchime, but more metallic. Mika turns and moves quickly in the other direction, away from the sound. But soon, the ringing can be heard again, very close, and she stiffens. Right in front of her in the fog is a figure. Mika can't see the face, just that the person is wearing a dirty dress and that she has a rope tied around her waist. From the rope hang a rusty pot and a tin mug. The hair stands up on the back of Mika's neck. It is Ragamuffin. The pot and the mug clank together when the figure comes closer. Mika wants to run away but she is immobilized by fear.

"So, Miss Uppity is back," a broken voice hisses. "Without the policeman here to protect her?"

From the fog appears a face with intense eyes and sharp cheekbones, framed by tangled hair. There are bruises around her neck in various shades of green. Mika realizes, for a dizzying moment, that she is looking at herself.

Mika can barely keep from screaming, but instead, what comes out of her mouth is a long moaning sound that causes the sleeping children in the dormitory to toss restlessly in their beds. The soaked sheet has twisted itself around her body like a straitjacket. Mika untangles herself and swings her legs over the edge of the bed. For a while, she just sits there and waits for her heart to calm down. Oh, how she regrets that she made Amelia tell her. Some things are better not known. For example, that your mother has

It was Axel's idea to switch the rubber bladder.

Then Cecilia, Nora's mother:

They arranged for me to go to a special place where somebody would help me have the baby.

For a few long seconds, Mika stands completely still; then she drops the mug in the bucket and hurries off down the hallway toward the office. The clock on the wall says almost midnight; the half round has not yet taken place. There's still time. Mika takes a piece of white paper from the pile that she has promised never to touch. The paper is for the records and Amelia's important letters only. But this is an emergency. Her hand trembles when she dips the tip of the pen in the inkwell.

> Beatrice,
> I know you are pregnant, and I know about the Dark Angel. I can help you. Please get in touch with me as soon as you can. Don't be afraid! Greetings from Mika Moonwind, Public Children's Home, Drottninggatan 73.

Mika runs through the sleeping orphanage on her bare feet. At the front door, she realizes that she is still wearing her nightgown. Very quietly, Mika makes her way back to the dormitory, picks up her pants and her shirt, and carefully closes the door behind her. She changes quickly in the antechamber and sneaks out through the front door. Heading south, toward Blasieholmen Island, she fills her lungs with tepid night air. In the pocket of her shirt is the rolled-up letter, just the right size to fit into a cigar case.

CHAPTER 22

The morning rain has turned Götgatan into a muddy mess, not unlike the floors of the Chapel on the weekends. The carriage jolts when one of the wheels hits a loose rock, and Valdemar grabs his chest, making a face.

"You drive like a carriage thief," he moans. "Speaking of which, where did you get that horse?"

"I borrowed it from the Priest's brewer's coachman," Mika replies. "The Chapel is a small bar, but we sell more beer than anyone else in all of Norrmalm. I told him a guest had died and we needed to take the body to the morgue. He didn't think that was strange at all."

Valdemar starts to laugh but his face immediately contorts with pain.

"Can you at least tell me where you're taking me," he pants.

"I've told you. A place where you won't have to fear being murdered in your sleep."

This does not seem to alleviate Valdemar's concerns. At Renstiernasgatan, a concerned wrinkle appears on his forehead, and when the carriage turns onto Stora Bondegatan, he stares at Mika in pure horror.

"Sweet Jesus, tell me we're not going where I think we are."

Mika gives Valdemar a stern look. "Is it better to be in your apartment, waiting to get murdered?"

"That's beginning to look like an attractive alternative," Valdemar mutters grumpily.

Next to the soap factory on Stora Bondegatan is an abandoned property surrounded by a large wooden fence. Farther back on the lot are a few outbuildings that look like they're about to fall down. Mika stops the carriage by the side of the road, ties the reins around a willow tree, and helps Valdemar down from the box seat. She moves a loose board in the fence, sticks her hand in the opening, and opens the gate. Then she looks at Valdemar.

"You'd better take your hat off, or somebody might take aim at it."

Valdemar grumbles a little, but in the end he does as he is told. Reluctantly, he follows Mika in through the gate. Together, they walk through the waist-high grass toward the farthest outbuilding. When they arrive, Mika knocks three times on the door, waits, then knocks two more times. That's the signal. They soon hear the metallic sound of a lock and the door swings open. A familiar figure stands on the threshold, dressed in a wide-brimmed stonemason's hat and an old military coat.

"I could say *welcome*," Tekla says, and lobs a wad of spittle over Valdemar's head. "But I don't like lying."

Valdemar turns to go back to the carriage but Mika grabs his arm and shoves him through the door. The building smells like a mix of coffee, tobacco, explosives, and old sweat. The shades have been pulled down and the only light comes from a flickering oil lamp in the ceiling. In the middle of the room is an old door on sawhorses, serving as a table. Four young women around the age of eighteen, all of them dressed a lot like Tekla, sit around the table. Mika has met most of the members of the Girls—Dina-mite, Neve the Knife, Jody Explode-y, and Nitro-Nellie—but she has never seen them all gathered in one place. They stare at Valdemar, whose eyes are roaming.

After a while Neve the Knife asks, "What kind of knife was it?"

Valdemar gives her a blank stare. "What?"

"That you were stabbed with, of course." Neve sighs. "Was it a butcher knife, a hunting knife, a bayonet, or a dagger? Did it have a single or a double edge?"

"Ah . . . I think it was just a regular dagger," Valdemar replies.

"There's the problem right there," Neve says, pursing her lips. "With a dagger, you can't just stab, you need to hit the heart. They should have twisted the knife to make the wound bigger, then you would have bled to death in two minutes."

"But in an apartment, blood might trickle down to the neighbor," Dina-mite points out. "They could have used a marline to strangle him instead."

"A thicker rope, rather," Nellie says, measuring Valdemar with her eyes. "He's too fat for a marline."

"The safest thing is a perfectly dosed charge," says Jody Explode-y. "Then you don't risk leaving any evidence for the police."

Valdemar gives Mika a look full of reproach. "You said I'd be safe here?"

"Safer than in the hospital," Tekla says. "If a rumor starts going around that somebody is trying to catch the Dark Angel, that person has one foot in the grave and the other in a bucket of dung. We're taking a huge risk protecting you."

She turns to Mika. "I hope you have a plan. We can't have a cop living here for very long; it's against our business model."

"Maybe," Mika says.

"Doris is waiting for you," Tekla says, nodding toward the door. "Just don't ask her what she's up to."

"This is a cesspool for criminals," Valdemar mutters, but Mika pretends not to hear him.

The sunlight hurts her eyes when she comes outside. Farther on, in the direction of the factory, is a smaller outbuilding with crooked walls and a wood-shingled roof. It looks abandoned, but Mika knows that things are not always the way they seem. She approaches gingerly, her arms overhead, palms up. Even though there is no sign of life, Mika knows that she's being watched. When she reaches the little staircase, the door swings open by itself. Inside, in the semidarkness, is a short woman with intense eyes and a kerchief tied around her hair. In her hands is a sawed-off shotgun. When she sees Mika, she takes her finger off the trigger.

"It's you, Mika. Come inside."

Mika has not seen Doris since last spring when Doris let her borrow a lockpick to break into Henrietta's apartment. Back then, Doris had a large model of a safe in her house. Now the floor is taken up by a strange contraption that reminds Mika of a diver's suit, entirely made from metal. Mika is just about to ask about it when she remembers Tekla's words and stops. Something about Doris feels unpredictable.

"I heard you wanted to talk to me," Doris says and puts her gun on the construction bench.

Mika hesitates. Then she blurts it out. "Tekla said you've been at Konradsberg."

Doris looks at her with a steady gaze. "I have an illness that makes me lose control sometimes. I'm not ashamed of it. Why are you interested in Konradsberg?"

"When I last met you, you said I looked familiar."

Doris knits her eyebrows. "What do you mean?"

"I have never met my parents," Mika continues. "The only thing I know is that my last name is Moonwind."

Doris's eyes light up. She approaches Mika slowly, until she is standing right in front of her; they are almost the same height. Gently, she touches Mika's hair and moves her fingertips along her jawline, like Nora does sometimes. Then she smiles with recognition.

"That's why you seemed so familiar. You're Annie's daughter."

Mika feels as if her heart might stop. *Annie. I have a mother and her name is Annie.*

"Is she there?" Mika whispers. "Is she still at Konradsberg?"

"Annie was only committed for three months. Then the doctors released her. The family she worked for had her committed against her will. She told me that she had given birth to a girl but had not been allowed to keep her." Doris looks at Mika, awed. "That's you, then."

"What was the name of the family she worked for?" Mika asks, excited. "Did she tell you my father's name?"

"Oh," Doris says and shakes her head. "It was so many years ago, and even though Annie and I became friends, we haven't been in touch since then. I tried to recruit her for a job. But, in case you're wondering, she wasn't like me."

"How do you mean?" Mika asks.

"Incorrigibly criminal."

On her way home, Mika can barely focus on driving. She scarcely notices the other coachmen ringing their bells at her, irritated. She may have a mother! A mother named Annie, who is not locked up in a mental hospital. Even though many of the puzzle pieces are still missing, this is more than she has ever dared hope for. Mika returns the brewer's wagon to Grönwall's Brewery and runs the rest of the way back to the orphanage.

In the entryway, she meets Rufus.

"Where have you been all morning?" he says. "Somebody is here waiting for you."

"Who?" Mika asks and immediately gets ready to flee.

Even though she didn't say her name at the building site, many people have seen her with Valdemar, both on Sibyllegatan and at Sabbatsberg Hospital.

"A girl," Rufus replies. "She didn't introduce herself, but she looks clean."

"What do you mean, *clean*?" Mika asks, irritated.

"You know what I mean," Rufus says. "She's just another kind."

Mika shakes her head as she walks down the hallway. But when she enters the kitchen, she understands what Rufus meant. On the bench sits a serious-looking girl with a nicely ironed dress and neat braids.

Hedvig von Denckert.

CHAPTER 23

Hedvig's eyes move from Mika's messy hair to her muddy boots.

"The last time we met, you lied to me," she says. "How do I know you won't lie now?"

"It was more of a bluff," Mika says, defending herself. "You would never have agreed to talk to me otherwise. And you actually lied first—to Constable Hoff."

Hedvig tilts her head. "There's a difference. Constable Hoff is working for the Douglas family. I had to lie to protect Beatrice."

"Valdemar would never do anything to hurt Beatrice," Mika says. "And this isn't just about her. You know what I mean."

Hedvig chews on her lip. "Swear," she demands. "Swear on the life of your family and everything you own that you're not lying."

"I can't," Mika replies. "I don't know if my family is alive, and I don't own anything but these clothes. But I swear on my life. It's worth as much as anybody else's."

Hedvig is quiet for a moment. Then she stands up and walks past Mika, toward the hallway. In the doorway, she turns around.

"Come on, then."

They walk south, through the bustling farmers market on Hötorget Square and down toward Hamngatan. Mika's leaky boots make a squelching sound, but Hedvig miraculously manages to avoid the horse manure, as well as the mud that splashes from the carriage wheels. As if she really were another kind, like Rufus said. Hedvig leads the way to a large house on Östra Trädgårdsgatan, right next to the King's Garden. In the entryway, they meet an older woman who measures Mika with her eyes.

"And who might this be?" the woman asks suspiciously.

"This is my classmate, Mika," Hedvig replies quickly. "I'm helping her with her homework."

Mika curtsies without making eye contact with the woman.

"That's our housekeeper," Hedvig says apologetically after the woman leaves. "She is nice, actually."

"You're a bad liar," Mika says. "Does anybody in your school look like me?"

A smile flickers across Hedvig's face. "No."

They continue down the hallway and through a corridor that leads to a courtyard. In one corner is a smaller building that reminds Mika of a custodian's living quarters. The shutters are closed, and the little house looks abandoned. Hedvig looks around, on guard, then takes a key from her dress pocket and inserts it in the lock.

They enter. The small building consists of a kitchen and a bedroom. Inside, the only light comes from what few thin rays manage to squeeze their way in between the shutters. When her eyes adjust to the dark, Mika notices a girl sitting on a bed. The girl has dark hair, almond-shaped eyes, and a big belly protruding under her nightgown. Other than the belly, Beatrice Douglas looks like her photograph.

"Who are you?" Beatrice asks shyly.

"I'm Mika," Mika replies.

"I understand that," Beatrice says with a voice that sounds breathless even though she's just been sitting there on the bed. "But how can you know about . . . everything?"

"This may sound strange," Mika says, "but I help the police sometimes. I was there when Constable Hoff interviewed your parents."

Beatrice snorts. "*Parents.* You know nothing."

"You're right, I don't know much for sure," Mika replies. "But I am guessing that Mrs. Douglas is not your real mother. And I know that you had consumption when you were four. If a child gets that, at least one of the parents usually does too. Like you, your mother survived, but the illness weakened her much more than it did you. I'd guess her pregnancy with Valter became too much, and she either died from childbirth or shortly thereafter. I'm sorry about that."

Beatrice doesn't move. The silence in the little room is so overwhelming that it feels almost unbearable. Mika holds her breath. When nobody else speaks, she continues. "I saw your room and I saw what your brother wrote, about Ivar and about your family wanting you to take a trip. I'm guessing it meant to the Dark Angel."

Beatrice looks at Mika for what feels like an eternity. Finally, she nods.

"Before he was let go, Ivar worked as a valet and a carriage driver at our house. Father and Marianne would never allow him to become a part of the family. For them, the child is just an unwanted heir. That's why they want to send me to the Dark Angel and have her deal with it. That's what they said: *deal with it.* As if I wouldn't understand what that meant."

Beatrice's eyes shine in the dark room.

"I don't know what to do," she says desperately. "I wanted us to hide at Ivar's parents' house, but they didn't dare. They're too afraid of Father. Ivar is also afraid, even though he pretends he's not. The child will come anytime, and I need to be out of here by then."

"My parents don't know that Betty is here," Hedvig explains.

Mika sits on the edge of the bed. "I have a suggestion," she says.

Beatrice shakes her head. "I'm sorry, but the only thing I know about you is that you're an orphan who works for the police. What do you want with me?"

"That is exactly what I am," Mika says. "And in the beginning, it was all about finding you. But it's not about that anymore. Valdemar and I want to stop the Dark Angel."

Beatrice lets out a hollow laugh. "Do you seriously think that you can do that? In that case, you have no idea who the Dark Angel is. Just asking questions about her will get you in trouble. And we don't even know each other. Why should I listen to you?"

"Because we need each other," Mika replies. "You want to save your child, and I want to catch the Dark Angel. Without each other's help we can't do either of those things."

Beatrice suddenly gasps and touches her belly, as if the baby kicked.

"What are you suggesting?" she asks.

"When we're finished talking, you will go straight home to your family. You will tell them that you agree to their terms, and that you will let them take you to the Dark Angel."

Beatrice looks dumbfounded.

"But what will really happen is something entirely different," Mika continues.

Then she shares her plan, the one nobody knows about, not even Valdemar or Tekla. She isn't totally sure about all the details yet.

When Mika is done, a tear runs down Beatrice's cheek. "How can you ask this of me?" she whispers. "How can I put my life and the life of my baby in your hands?"

"Because we're your only chance," Mika replies honestly. "Either the Dark Angel gets your baby, or you will have to live in hiding with a baby."

Beatrice's eyes dart around the room. Hedvig takes her hand.

"This didn't start with you," Mika continues. "But it will end here. We have to try. If we don't, more children will die."

Even in the dark, Mika can tell that Beatrice's face is white.

"When?" she whispers. "When will we do it?"

Mika tries to think. There is no time to lose. If the baby arrives, it will be too late. But she needs time to persuade Valdemar and Tekla.

"Seven o'clock tomorrow night."

For a long time, Beatrice sits quietly with Hedvig's hand in hers. Then she looks at Mika and nods resolutely.

"Yes, I'll do it."

CHAPTER 24

Mika is standing outside Tekla's shed. She has knocked the secret signal twice, but nobody opens. From the other side of the door, she hears loud voices. She hears Valdemar, and it sounds like he's screaming. *What if they're killing him?* Mika thinks, appalled. Even if he was healthy and armed, Valdemar would not stand a chance against Tekla. Mika finally opens the door herself even though she knows it might be dangerous. A smell of bouillon and fried onions wafts toward her. The Girls are gathered around the table, eating while they listen to Valdemar, who is right in the middle of a story.

". . . and when I pulled him out of the chimney, he was entirely naked, still holding the squirrel in his hand."

Everybody around the table is in stitches, laughing.

"What are you doing?" Mika asks.

"This cop can cook," Dina-mite says, pointing at Valdemar with her spoon, her mouth full of hash and eggs.

"We might keep him," Nitro-Nellie says.

"Tekla's cop hotel," Tekla says, as if she could just see the sign in front of her. "Frog legs and Chateau Brian, or whatever that was on the menu."

Mika is still standing in the doorway. "I know how to find the Dark Angel," she says.

The chatting and the ruckus end immediately, and the room turns quiet. Everybody looks at Mika. Tekla licks the grease from her knife and puts it back in her boot.

"Let's hear it."

Mika tells them what she told Beatrice. When she's finished, six people stare at her as if she has lost her mind. Nellie pushes her plate away, making a face. Nobody is hungry anymore.

"Beatrice Douglas is going along with this?" Valdemar asks skeptically.

"She doesn't have a choice," Mika replies. "This is her only chance to keep the baby."

"What's in it for us?" Jody asks.

With a bang, Tekla turns the table over, sending plates and mugs flying across the floor. Her eyes shine with anger when she jumps up and pushes Jody against the wall.

"Who the hell do you think you're talking to?" she hisses between clenched teeth. "I have known Mika longer than I have known any of you. She comes from the Public, never forget that."

"Let go of me!" Jody wrestles herself free and glares angrily at Tekla.

"You have helped me and Valdemar before," Mika says. "But this isn't about us. The Dark Angel is the worst murderer in the history of this city. It doesn't matter if you're a policeman, a stonemason, a criminal, or an orphan—if we have a chance to stop her, we have to take it."

Tekla watches the quiet group. "What did you think? That we would grow old like this? People like us either end up in the grave before we're twenty-five, or in jail. Mika is right, this is bigger than us."

Jody Explode-y, Dina-mite, Nitro-Nellie, and Neve the Knife exchange looks.

"I'm not twisting anybody's arm," Tekla says quietly. "But whoever doesn't want to be a part of this can take their belongings and leave right now."

A tense silence fills the shack. After a few seconds that seem to last forever, Jody sighs and says, "Count me in."

The rest of the Girls nod their assent.

"I'm sick of life anyway," Nellie adds, and just like that, the tension is broken and the gang bursts out laughing.

Valdemar shakes his head, resigned.

"You seem to have made some new friends," Mika says, sitting outside the building with Valdemar a little later.

Valdemar looks over his shoulder to make sure nobody is listening.

"Those people are completely insane," he hisses. "I got no sleep last night because somebody was sharpening knives, probably Neve. When I finally managed to fall asleep at dawn, I woke up from somebody accidentally setting off a gun. The shot went through the wall three inches above my head. They belong in prison, every last one of them."

The match trembles between Valdemar's fingers when he lights his pipe and takes a winded puff. He gives Mika a questioning look. "Are you sure you want to do this?"

"No," Mika replies honestly. "But it's the only idea I have."

"How did you come up with it?" Valdemar asks.

Mika shrugs. "By accident. I discovered that a few of the children were stealing sweets. They had taken the rubber insert from a soccer ball and filled the shell with chocolate. A few days later, Nora's mother told me that her fiancé's parents had planned to take her to the Dark Angel. The location was secret, but a carriage would be sent to pick her up."

"We switch the contents of the carriage, and nobody will know the difference," Valdemar says slowly. "Brilliant, I have to say. Not to mention insanely dangerous."

He coughs and touches his chest, making a face.

"I'm still weak from the loss of blood. I'm afraid I won't be much help if things turn violent."

"*If*," Mika repeats with a crooked smile.

She meets Valdemar's gaze. They both know that tomorrow will be violent. The Girls know it too. Mika saw it in Tekla's eyes: the extraordinary hunger for violence that she cannot understand.

"If we get through this, I'm done with death," Mika says firmly.

Valdemar leans against the wall and looks at the sun.

"I used to think like that, too, when I was younger. That he was an unwelcome companion that you could shake off."

"You say *he*," Mika points out. "How do you know that death is a man?"

"I didn't say he was a man."

A cloud moves across the sky, and Valdemar follows the thin shadow with his eyes as it sweeps across the sunburned meadow, rolls over the wooden fence, and disappears along Stora Bondegatan.

"Days before I got the news about Silas, I saw a dog sitting in the yard at dusk. There was something strangely familiar about him, something that I couldn't put my finger on." The tobacco makes a soft rustling sound when Valdemar takes a deep puff. He lets the smoke waft out between his brown teeth.

"Before I joined the police force, I worked in the military for a long time. I've seen crime scenes and accidents that I prefer to forget. Once, seven of my friends died in an explosion in a grenade storage. Later, I noticed a starved dog sneaking around among the ruins, a dirty yellow color, tangled fur. Not until after Silas's funeral did I understand that what I'd seen was death."

Mika doesn't want to ask, but she does anyway. "When did you last see the dog?"

Valdemar doesn't look; he just points with the shaft of his pipe toward a small copse of linden trees in the corner of the yard.

"He's over there in the grass. It looks like he's asleep, but he never is."

From far away, a factory whistle can be heard. A group of men walk across the factory yard, and behind them, a lone girl. *The girl looks like Hanna,* Mika thinks, the factory girl who told her about Klara Lind and helped solve the mystery of the Night Raven. She hopes she's wrong, and that Hanna has found other work.

"I want to ask you a favor," Valdemar says, hesitating. "The skeletons are still there, in the winter grave at Sankt Johannes Cemetery. Regardless of what happens tomorrow, those children should have a proper funeral."

He takes a folded piece of paper from his pocket and hands it to Mika. "Tomorrow, ask your houseparent to lock this letter away overnight. If I don't make it, please tell her to read it. And if you . . ."

He doesn't need to finish the sentence. Mika understands.

"I promise."

They sit together in silence and watch the trees' shadows slowly grow longer. From Doris's shack comes the sound of hammer on metal. Mika suddenly remembers something that Amelia said:

The Dark Angel was supposed to get you.

Despite the heat, a cold shiver moves up Mika's spine. She hasn't thought about it until now, but it sounds like a prophecy.

CHAPTER 25

Amelia holds Valdemar's letter in her hand and glares at Mika over the frames of her glasses.

"Until tomorrow?" she repeats.

Mika nods. "It's nothing. Just in case."

Amelia doesn't look convinced. But she puts the letter in the archive cabinet, closes the hatch, and turns the key. Then she starts working, pretending that she can't see Mika still lingering in her office.

"I'm not going to ask what this is about," Amelia says finally. "If that's what you're waiting for. Because you won't tell me anyway."

"That's not it," Mika says slowly. "I wonder . . . if you could braid my hair."

Amelia looks puzzled. "You never wear braids."

"I know," Mika says. "But now I want to."

From her pocket, she takes a picture of Beatrice Douglas, and puts it on the desk. "Like this."

A shadow moves across Amelia's face. She stares into Mika's eyes without even looking at the photograph.

"You come and go as you please," she says, her teeth clenched. "Disappear for days and leave me with the responsibility of the entire orphanage, without even telling me what you're up to. Don't you think I know what that letter is about? You . . ."

Her voice disappears suddenly, like when a drowning person is pulled under the surface, and she has to catch her breath before she can continue. "You demand that I sit here and wait for you to maybe return. And now you want me to braid your hair?"

Without waiting for an answer, Amelia storms out of the office and slams the door behind her. Mika stays behind, confused. Just as she's about to leave, Amelia is back, a brush in her hand.

"Sit."

Roughly, Amelia brushes through the tangled hair. When the brush gets stuck in a snarl, she yanks so hard that Mika's head is pulled back. The pain makes Mika's eyes tear up. But no way is she going to say something; she'd rather Amelia pull all her hair out, roots and all. As the snarls get brushed out, Amelia's movements grow calmer.

When Mika's hair is combed through, Amelia parts it in the middle and divides one side into three thick strands that she pinches between her thumb, her index finger, and her long finger. Softly and methodically, Amelia begins braiding Mika's hair. Now and then, she pauses to move some hair, or gather up some that doesn't want to stay where it's supposed to. When both braids are finished, she carefully ties them with a string. Amelia has never been one to touch children unnecessarily but now she lets her hand rest on Mika's neck, rough and warm. Out in the yard, the wind has gotten hold of a paper bag. The bag swirls around in a circle on the ground until it is sucked up in the air and disappears out of sight. A sudden gust makes the windowpanes rattle.

"A storm is brewing, my girl," Amelia says quietly.

Mika nods. "I know."

With a sigh, Amelia puts the brush in her pocket and disappears out the door. Left on her desk is the photograph of Beatrice. Mika looks at her own mirror image in the window. The hairstyle is exactly the same.

I am the storm.

CHAPTER 26

The gray sky weighs heavily over Blasieholmen Island—threatening, like a water-filled balloon that might burst at any moment. From the roof of the Grand Hotel comes the clanking of the halyard ropes against the flagpoles. Below, waves propel themselves angrily against the quay. Outside the door of Arsenalsgatan 4, a carriage is parked, the words MALMSTEN'S TILE printed on its tarp. On the box seat sits a thin figure dressed in stonemason's pants and a military coat, reclining comfortably, feet on the footrest and a slouch hat pulled down over the forehead. From each of the boot shafts, the handles of two knives stick out. From a distance, it looks as if the figure is asleep, but beneath the brim of the hat glows a pair of green eyes, trained on the gray building at the north end of Blasieholmen Island. When a white curtain is pulled on the second window of the third floor, Tekla sits up on the box seat. She knocks on the side of the carriage with the handle of her whip.

"There's the signal," she announces.

Inside the carriage, Valdemar pulls out his watch. "Seven sharp," he says. "It has begun."

The first step of the plan is for Beatrice to pretend that her contractions have begun, to convince her family that the baby is on its way. It seems to be working because soon, the front door to the Douglas family's house opens and a young man in a servant's uniform runs west along Arsenalsgatan.

"Can't we just follow him?" Mika asks impatiently.

"Most likely, the boy only has the address 0f the closest middleman," Valdemar explains. "Theoretically, we could follow the middleman. But it's too risky. If it's a single man on a horse, we could easily lose him."

He looks at his watch again. "We have approximately half an hour before the next step begins. Are you ready?"

Mika nods and tries to calm her breathing. She is wearing clothes that she borrowed from Beatrice—a long, dark-blue dress with a black-hooded coat. Under the dress, she has a tightly stuffed pillow, to make her stomach look like Beatrice's. There's a knock on the carriage door. It's Nitro-Nellie.

"Are the charges in place?" Valdemar asks.

"Half a kilo of white phosphorous in every direction," Nellie assures him. "The smoke screen will take full effect in a few seconds. But the wind is a problem; don't count on more than a minute's delay."

"Understood," Valdemar replies in a military manner.

Nellie reaches toward Mika, her hands cupped, as if she's holding a newly hatched chicken.

"Take this," she whispers. "But don't drop it, whatever you do."

Mika looks quizzically at the item that Nellie gives her. In her hand is a ball of glued paper scraps, approximately the size of an apple.

"What is it?"

"It is a weak mix of gunpowder," Nellie replies. "Inside it is an igniter that gets activated by a heavy blow. The explosion will create a wave large enough to eliminate anybody within a ten-yard radius. I've never made anything like this before, and I'm not sure about the dose. Use it only in the utmost emergency, when there is no other solution."

She puts a hand on Mika's arm. "Do you understand?"

Mika nods. There is no mistaking the seriousness in Nellie's eyes. Carefully, she puts the paper ball in her dress pocket. The minute hand on Valdemar's watch moves very slowly. They wait in silence. Close to seven thirty, something happens. From Östra Trädgårdsgatan, a carriage approaches, pulled by two burly horses. The covered wagon looks like a detention carriage, but without the barred windows. This carriage has no windows at all. The coachman is dressed in a coat, a hat, and a black scarf that hides everything but his eyes. Tekla looks demonstratively uninterested and, as the carriage passes, she spits a wad of snuff on the sidewalk. The coachman tightens his reins and stops in front of the Douglas family home.

"Give the first signal," Valdemar commands.

Tekla raises the long whip in the air to announce to the Girls that the carriage has arrived. Four roads lead out of Blasieholmen Island. Nitro-Nellie and Dina-mite are watching each end of Stallgatan, while Jody Explode-y and Neve the Knife are in charge of Arsenalsgatan. The only question is, which way will the carriage take?

Mika feels her heart hammer in her chest as she looks out through a gap in the tarp. After a while, Beatrice appears in the doorway. She walks stooped over, propping herself on her father's arm, as if she's in pain. Mr. Douglas opens the door to the carriage and helps Beatrice in. From the window on the third floor, Valter and Hedvig von Denckert look down on them. The distance makes it impossible to know for sure, but it seems as if Hedvig is looking right at Mika. Down in the street, Mr. Douglas is making sure that the carriage door is locked. Then he gives the coachman a nod.

Mika lifts the hood of her coat and gets ready. The coachman snaps his reins and the carriage cuts across the square.

"They're taking Stallgatan south," Valdemar concludes. "Give the signal!"

Tekla signs to Dina-mite, who signals to Nitro-Nellie. Then she disengages the brakes and snaps the whip in the air. The horse takes off immediately, so fast that Mika and Valdemar have to hold on. The moment that the carriage turns the corner, they see that Nellie's charge has worked; Stallgatan's south entrance is entirely hidden behind a thick, impenetrable smoke cloud.

"Fire!" somebody calls, and the pedestrians along the street look around, confused, trying to locate the fire.

The black carriage is stuck in the middle of the street. The coachman fights to control his horses, which are trying to back away from the smoke, but to no avail. Tekla parks across the street, to block the way back. When the Girls come running and swing themselves up on the cargo bed, Mika jumps out and runs in a crouch toward the black carriage, careful to stay out of the coachman's field of vision. When she reaches the carriage, she stays behind it, her back to it. When Tekla gives the all-clear sign, Mika makes her way around to the carriage's right side. She has Doris's lockpick in her pocket, but she doesn't need to use it because the carriage door has only a simple latch. Just as Mika is about to lift the latch, the coachman turns around. Mika's heart flies up in her throat and she hides under the carriage. The large wheels rock back and forth as the horses pull at their shafts. If one of them should roll over Mika, it would all be over. She makes eye contact with Tekla, who mimes, *Now!*

In one swift movement, Mika pulls herself up on the foothold, pushes the latch up, and opens the door. She takes Beatrice's hand and helps her down into the street. Then Mika sits in the carriage herself. Before the door closes, she whispers, "Wait at Hedvig's house for a few hours before you return home. Now, lock me up."

There is a rustling sound from the lock when Beatrice puts the latch back. Then it gets quiet. *Too* quiet. Mika holds her breath while she waits for the coachman to fling open the door and discover her. But nothing happens. Just as the lack of oxygen begins to hurt, the carriage starts swaying again and rolls on. Mika takes a breath and fills her lungs with air. It worked.

She is on her way to the Dark Angel.

CHAPTER 27

In the thick darkness, everything turns remarkably still. The only sound is Mika's own breathing, and the soft clip-clop from the hooves on the cobblestones. She listens for clues that might tell her where they are, like church bells or a different type of pavement. The carriage is traveling west on Strömgatan, so they should be at Norrmalm by now. Or did they turn at the Norrbro bridge? In that case, they are on Stadsholmen Island. The sense of having no control tightens like a noose around Mika's neck. She tries to focus on breathing calmly and on the fact that she's not alone, that Valdemar and the Girls are following behind in their carriage.

After about ten minutes, the carriage stops. Soon, she hears the click from the latch and the door opens. Even though the sky is overcast, Mika is blinded by the light. When her eyes adjust, she sees that the carriage has been parked very close to a door. In the doorway stands a woman in her thirties, wearing a dress and a white apron, almost like the nurses at Sabbatsberg Hospital.

"Come, Miss Douglas," the woman says, holding out her hand. "I will help you."

Mika had hoped for a better overview of her surroundings, but the carriage is so close to the wall of the building that she can't see what street they're on. *To make sure I won't be able to escape,* she thinks. In the small gap between the house and the carriage, she glimpses a slope going down to the water. It might be one of the alleys that leads down to Skeppsbron Bridge. Not Ferkens, because it is vaulted. But possibly Drakens or Skottgränd. Mika cannot see anything else before the woman with the apron pulls her across the threshold and closes the door.

The woman brings Mika up a vaulted stone staircase. On the second floor, a man stands in front of a closed door. Mika notices both a gun and a knife in his belt. The coachman, she noticed, has stayed outside. That means at least two guards. The man nods at the woman with the apron and opens the door. Inside is a rectangular room, approximately the size of Valdemar's apartment. All the windows are covered; the light comes from oil lamps that shine yellow on the furnishings—a simple cot covered only by a sheet, a bench on wheels, and an empty zinc washbasin.

The woman brings Mika in over the threshold and the guard closes the door behind them. Mika feels panic starting to scratch inside of her, wanting out.

"Sit down on the cot," the woman instructs. "I will help you with your shoes."

Before Mika can do anything, the woman has taken off one of her boots. She looks at the boot, surprised. After hesitating for a second, she takes off the other boot as well. Mika swears inside. She should have borrowed a pair of shoes from Beatrice. A girl like Beatrice would never walk around barefoot in a pair of boots full of holes.

"Lie down, please," the woman says, putting her arm behind Mika's back to help her.

The cot is hard and cold. *Where are you, Valdemar?* Mika thinks. To calm herself, she watches the dancing flames of the oil lamps making patterns in the ceiling. The woman with the apron is putting a pile of clean towels on the bench and pouring scalding-hot water from a cauldron. Mika wonders if she's mistaken. The woman is so young; can she really be the Dark Angel? Or is she one of many? Then she hears a creaking sound, as if somebody is standing up from a chair. At that moment, Mika realizes they're not alone in the room. She slowly turns her head in the direction of the sound. Farther into the room, beyond the reach of the lamps, she sees the outline of a short figure. At first,

Mika thinks it is a child. Then the figure steps into the light and Mika feels the hairs on the back of her neck stand up.

It's difficult to determine the age of the woman who has just freed herself from the shadows, but despite her straight posture and her sinewy body, she must be at least eighty. The skin on her face is as shiny as a horse's saddle and stretched tightly over sharp cheekbones. The silver-gray hair has been gathered in a tidy bun. Even though Mika is lying down, the woman's narrow eyes give her vertigo—two bottomless wells of endless darkness. It is not evil that Mika perceives, but rather some kind of dark, ancient force, animal-like. Mika feels a chill seep into the room, making its way in through her skin, spreading with her blood to her very heart.

The Dark Angel.

The younger woman picks up a notebook, turns to a page, and reads out loud: "Beatrice Douglas, daughter of Charles Douglas and stepdaughter of Marianne Douglas of Blasieholmstorg Square 12. Somewhat lowered lung capacity since the age of four, otherwise fully healthy. Payment has been taken care of."

"Don't worry, Miss Douglas," says the Dark Angel with a surprisingly light voice. "This will soon be over. If you want to address me, you can just call me 'Ma'am.' When we're done, the carriage will bring you home and you can forget that we ever met."

Mika nods. On the bench is a tray with hospital instruments—clamps, scalpels, and large forceps.

"When did your contractions begin?" the Dark Angel asks.

She sits down on the cot and puts her hands on Mika's stomach. Her gnarled fingers move across the dress fabric like the legs of an insect. Mika squeezes her eyes shut. *Please, Valdemar, come now,* she thinks. *Come now come now come now.* At that moment, the Dark Angel stiffens. Without a warning, she pushes so hard with her thumbs that Mika gasps.

"What's wrong?" the woman with the apron asks, confused.

For a few trembling seconds, the room is entirely silent. Then the Dark Angel calls out.

"Kronwall!"

"Ma'am."

"Hold the girl," the Dark Angel orders.

The guard immediately comes over and pushes Mika's arms down. The Dark Angel reaches for an oil lamp. She holds the lamp in front of her while she lifts Mika's upper lip with her thumb. Her eyes narrow when she sees her teeth.

"This is no Douglas," she hisses to the younger woman. "This is a street rat with a pillow under her dress. What's going on?"

Then, from the floor below, comes a ruckus—loud voices and the sound of a fight. The Dark Angel walks over to the window, opens the curtain a little, and looks down in the street. She turns to the guard.

"The carriage was followed," she says, her voice constrained. "Kronwall must take us out of here as soon as possible. But get rid of the girl first."

The young woman immediately gathers the instruments from the bench and hurries to the door. The guard lifts Mika roughly.

"Put her in the tub," the Dark Angel instructs.

Mika's blood freezes in her veins when she understands what they are about to do. Desperate, she tries to get away, but the guard's grip is like a vice. Out of the corner of her eye, Mika sees the Dark Angel disappear out the door. Then the guard throws her in the tub, goes down on his knees, and pins her down by holding his left arm across her chest. The air is squeezed out of her lungs and she can't even scream. The guard pulls a long, narrow blade from his boot, and Mika stops fighting. It's over. She understands that. She closes her eyes and thinks about her favorite place—sitting next to Valdemar on the box seat, the sun in her face and Rutger between the shafts, heading out on assignment. Then Mika remembers what Nellie gave her. She fumbles in her dress pocket with her free hand until her fingers close around the little ball. As the guard puts his blade to Mika's throat, Mika throws the paper ball as hard as she can. There is a crackling sound from the igniter when the ball hits the wall. Surprise fills the guard's eyes; then he is lifted to the ceiling by an invisible hand and thrown across the room. The pressure wave hits Mika like the kick of a horse. Helplessly, she falls down toward a lake as calm as a mirror. Her body breaks the surface and beneath it, there is nothing, just soft, forgiving darkness.

Mika's last thought is that death feels like the hug of a mother.

CHAPTER 28

Mika sinks slowly into soft nothingness. Somewhere high above, she sees a billowing surface and concerned faces. A soft sound keeps cutting into the nothingness—somebody calling her name. Her cheek smarts, as if from a slap, and Mika is propelled up toward the surface.

She is not at the bottom of a lake after all, but in the back of Tekla's carriage. The billowy surface she saw was the flapping tarp of the carriage roof. The concerned faces were those of Nitro-Nellie, Neve the Knife, and Dina-mite. Mika suddenly realizes how much everything hurts. Her body aches as if she has been beaten up by somebody very large and very angry. And her face stings in a strange way, as if she has been burnt by the sun. The members of the Girls look pretty messed up too. The left side of Nitro-Nellie's jaw looks scratched and swollen, as if from a hard punch. Neve the Knife's shirt is soaked in blood from her nose, which looks like it's been broken. Jody Explode-y sits on the box seat with the reins in one hand, the other arm hanging loose by her side, as if out of joint.

"Clvr wi tb," Nellie says.

"What?" Mika says, confused.

After the explosion, there is a constant ringing in her ears.

"Clever with the tub!" Nellie calls. "If you hadn't been in there, you might not have made it."

"I was in the tub because they were going to cut me open," Mika says emphatically. "What took you so long?"

"We stopped for a picnic," Dina says and spits a wad of blood in the street. "What does it look like?"

"The place was better guarded than we thought," Neve says placatingly. "Judging from the resistance and the equipment, the guards were former military. But they ran away when you set off your charge."

"The guard who was in the room with you survived but was too battered to get away. The police probably have him by now. The explosion blew out every window on the second floor."

The cobblestones on Lilla Bondegatan make for a bumpy ride and Mika feels a stabbing in her ribs.

"What happened to the Dark Angel?" she tries, carefully. "Is she alive?"

"Your work is done," Dina says dismissively. "Don't worry about the Dark Angel. Tekla and Valdemar took care of her."

It is a bedraggled crew that arrives at the shack. Mika has to lean on Nellie and Neve to even get up the tiny staircase.

"Try to stay awake," Dina says and hands Mika a cup of water. "You were hit pretty hard. If you fall asleep, you might swallow your tongue."

"No risk of that," Mika replies and drinks her water down in two deep gulps.

One by one, the Girls leave to clean up, but Mika really needs to rest a little. She crawls into a corner and lies down on top of some old newspapers. At that moment, it is as if somebody unloads a wagon of dirt on top of her. Her body is nailed to the floor and while the ringing in her ears slowly subsides, she slips into something between sleep and unconsciousness.

After what feels like many hours, Mika wakes to somebody touching her forehead with a rough board. It turns out to be Valdemar's hand. He is sitting on the floor with his back to the wall, breathing heavily, blood leaking from the bandage on his chest.

"Thank goodness you're alive, Ragamuffin."

"You weren't going to call me that," Mika slurs.

Valdemar looks chastised. "I'm sorry," he says.

"It's okay."

"I mean, I'm sorry I didn't get there on time," Valdemar says. "You went ahead with your part of the plan, but we failed. It could have ended badly."

"I've never felt better," Mika says, giving him a weak smile. "But I wonder how Beatrice is doing."

"We'll visit the Douglas family as soon as possible," Valdemar assures her. "But now that the Dark Angel is out of the game, Beatrice is safe for the moment."

Mika hardly dares ask. "*Out of the game.* Is she . . . ?"

"She's alive and in custody. Thanks to you."

"Where?" Mika asks.

"I didn't dare bring her to jail," Valdemar replies. "Many people pass through that jail and if any of the inmates recognized her, she might get murdered before she can stand trial."

Mika looks confused. "But if she's not in jail, where is she?"

Valdemar looks around as if to make sure they're alone. Then he lowers his voice.

"In the Rose Chamber."

Mika sits up, not sure that she heard him correctly.

"The Rose Chamber," she repeats skeptically. "You mean it's real?"

"Not officially," Valdemar replies. "But yes."

Every single kid at the Public Children's Home has heard of the Rose Chamber. A hundred years ago there was a prison called Nya Smedjegården, not far from the children's home. Beneath the prison was a horrible torture chamber where the prisoners were tormented until they confessed to their crimes. It was called the Rose Chamber. But Nya Smedjegården is long gone, replaced by Norrmalm Central Prison—a prison for women.

Mika stands up on wobbly legs.

"Sit down!" Valdemar says and reaches for her, but Mika slaps his hand away.

"I want you to listen to me," she says sternly. "I've earned it."

Valdemar leans his head against the wall. "I can't argue with that," he says. "What do you want?"

Mika looks him in the eyes without blinking.

"I want to meet her."

CHAPTER 29

Norrmalm Central Prison is located on one of the corners of Norra Bantorget Square, neighboring the Public Children's Home. On the other side of Klara Strandgata, in the direction of Barnhusviken Bay, towers the large Cellfängelset Prison—for men. Mika walks behind Valdemar through the entrance hall, which, with its tiny, barred windows facing out onto a bare prison yard, reminds her of a stable. Suddenly, a whistle sounds, one that Mika has heard so many times from a distance, and the yard begins to fill up with women of all ages. Mika looks at the gaunt faces. Would she recognize her own mother if she saw her?

Valdemar wipes a sweaty strand of hair from his forehead and buttons his shirt all the way up to hide the bandage. He walks up to a guard.

"Constable Hoff, Criminal Investigations Department of the Stockholm Police. I am here to visit Aunt Dagny."

The key chain jingles when the guard unlocks a door. He nods for them to follow.

"Aunt Dagny?" Mika mimes, but Valdemar pretends not to see her.

They walk along a corridor with rows of cell doors. The building is in the same bad condition as the orphanage, and a sharp smell of mold and rotten wood pierces her nose. Far down the hallway is a small alcove in the wall, with a low iron door.

"The cops are curious," says the young guard in a friendly manner, turning the key in the lock. "Who is she? Really?"

"Your cellmate, if you keep meddling in things that aren't your business," Valdemar snaps.

The young guard's smile disappears faster than a week's salary at the Chapel, and he quickly opens the door. On the other side, a narrow stone staircase leads down into the dark. Valdemar nods for Mika to follow him; then he ducks down under the low arch. For every step they take, the temperature falls. It reminds Mika of slowly walking into a lake in the spring.

"Aunt Dagny is a code name," Valdemar explains when the guard is out of earshot. "Not even the staff knows who she is, only the authorities. If rumors begin to go around that the police have the Dark Angel, heads will roll."

The basement ceiling is so low that Valdemar has to take his hat off to be able to stand up straight.

"The Rose Chamber has not been used for its original purpose since Nya Smedjegården closed and the new prison took over," he continues. "But that doesn't mean that it has ceased to exist. According to an old agreement between the police and the city prisons, the Rose Chamber may be used for cases that are sensitive for various reasons. During my time with the police, I have never heard of such a case."

Valdemar unhooks a lamp from the wall and adds, "Until today, that is."

"What will happen to her?" Mika asks.

"Tomorrow, the Dark Angel will be taken to the courthouse," Valdemar replies. "After sentencing, she will be moved immediately to an unnamed prison, where she will spend the rest of her life. When this reaches the public, it will already be over."

He gives Mika a somber look. "Are you sure you want to do this?"

Mika's entire body aches after the explosion. Her lungs feel tight and every breath hurts in her chest. Yet she nods. "I need to."

On the other side of a tiled vault is a rectangular room with no windows. The rough stone walls are shiny from the humidity, and from the ceiling hangs a lone oil lamp whose weak light scarcely reaches the corners of the room. Iron rings hang on the walls and a shallow gutter runs along the floor beneath them. The sight makes Mika shiver. Once upon a time, prisoners hung from these rings; they were tortured, suffering horrible pain, their blood gushing down into the gutter. Even if the events took place long ago, it's as if everything is still there in the very air. Beyond the oil lamp's puddle of light is a newer iron grate that divides the room in two, like a cage. For a few seconds, it is as quiet as it can only be in an underground stone basement. Then they hear a light voice.

"The street rat."

In the semidarkness on the other side of the grate is the Dark Angel. Her voice holds no surprise; it is a factual statement.

"I'm not a street rat," Mika says. "I live at the Public Children's Home."

"So, you were the worm that the police put on the hook to catch me," says the Dark Angel. "What did they lure you with? Food, money—promises of another life?"

"It was my idea," Mika says.

From the dark comes a low chuckle. "Girl, don't get any ideas. From the cradle to the grave, your life is in other people's hands."

"She's right," Valdemar says, but he stops when Mika raises her hand.

The Dark Angel steps closer to the bars. "Then you must have had a good reason. And I assume it is the same reason that you are standing here right now."

Mika takes a deep breath. "My mother was going to be sent to you twelve years ago, in August 1868. Her name was Annie Moonwind."

"I know I must seem like a monster to you," the Dark Angel says slowly. "But if I had added all my clients' names to my memory bank, it would have done me in a long time ago."

It is quiet again. A drop of water falls from the ceiling, causing the oil lamp to flutter. The Dark Angel's eyes glow in the dark.

"I have always thought that children don't have a chance," she says. "That I free them from a life as bastards, cast out from their own families. But you made it. And here you are, bossing a police officer around."

The Dark Angel takes another step toward the grate. "Come here, let me look at you."

"Mika . . . ," Valdemar warns.

Mika pretends not to hear him. Slowly, she walks across the floor toward the cage. In the semidarkness the old woman's face comes into clear view. Under the too-tightly-stretched skin, as thin as silk paper, her veins look like irregular pen marks. Gnarled hands grip the grate's iron bars, and the Dark Angel examines Mika from top to bottom.

"My ending has always been inevitable," she says eventually. "But I thought my executioner would look different."

"I'm not an executioner," Mika says. "I've never killed anybody, and I won't."

"I see that's what you want to believe," the Dark Angel says. "And I hope you won't have to. But I know what you are. We are more alike, you and I, than you realize. For most people, life is close and death is far away. That's not how it is with us. Death lives in our shadow; it is rarely far enough away that we can't smell it. People like *him*"—she nods disgustedly toward Valdemar—"have tried to catch me for half a century. I'm here because you were willing to risk your own life."

The sudden memory of the cold knife blade on her throat makes Mika shiver. She has not yet fully comprehended how close it was.

"Believe me, I wished for a different life too," the Dark Angel continues. "But once upon a time, my profession was given to me as a punishment. And we do whatever work is given to us. In the end, even the unthinkable can become a habit."

Her eyes are calm when they meet Mika's.

"As I said, I don't remember all my customers. But I remember things that stick out from the ordinary. Once, for example, I was told to get rid of a child, but when the day came the pregnant girl disappeared without a trace. But the boy's family was honorable, and I still got paid. They showed me and my profession respect. We agreed that I would finish the job later."

The Dark Angel's words make Mika's body go numb.

"What do you mean?" she asks.

The Dark Angel smiles, and her voice is almost mild when she says, "I didn't suspect back then that it would take twelve years."

Then everything happens very quickly. Without a warning, the Dark Angel propels herself forward, her arms shoot out through the bars, and the gnarled fingers seize Mika's wrists. Mika is pulled toward the bars and, when the Dark Angel opens her mouth, Mika can smell the odor from the black tooth stumps. The next moment, the basement is filled with Valdemar's booming voice.

"Let go of the girl!"

Valdemar rushes toward the cage, fumbling for his police stick. The Dark Angel lets go and Mika stumbles backward on the floor.

"Holy horror," Valdemar exclaims, examining Mika's face under the lamp. "Did she bite you?"

Mika shakes her head and shoves him away.

"I'm not injured," she mumbles. "But I want to leave. Now."

Together they walk toward the light trickling down the stairs. Mika tries to make sense of the thoughts rushing through her head. As soon as they get upstairs, she will tell Valdemar what really happened. The Dark Angel did not bite her. She whispered something.

A name.

CHAPTER 30

Mr. Douglas pours himself a glass of cognac. He gives Valdemar a quizzical look. Valdemar shakes his head.

"Not for me but thank you for the offer."

"Whoever resists a twenty-five-year-old Delamain either has bad judgment or a strong character," Mr. Douglas says and puts the carafe back on the serving cart. "I choose to believe the latter of you, Constable Hoff."

"The girl might want something," Mrs. Douglas says, looking at Mika, who is standing behind Valdemar, her back to the wall. "A glass of lemonade perhaps?"

"No, thank you. That's very kind, ma'am," Mika says with a quick curtsy.

Mr. Douglas looks flummoxed, as if he has not even noticed Mika. He picks up his glass and sits down on the couch next to his wife.

"According to Beatrice, the constable is to thank for the fact that she saw reason and returned home. My wife and I are very grateful for what you have done. And we would appreciate it if you would not disclose anything about Beatrice's . . . condition. Our wishes are that it stays in the family. Anything else might bring undesirable consequences for both us and you, as the constable surely understands."

"Entirely," Valdemar replies. He takes his pipe out of his pocket. "Please, excuse me."

Looking right into Mr. Douglas's eyes, Valdemar scratches out the contents of the pipe onto the floor. He carefully fills the pipe with new tobacco, lights a match on the striker, and takes a few deep puffs to get the embers going. Then he puts the still smoking match on the shiny surface of the table.

"It's not official yet," Valdemar says, putting one leg comfortably over the other. "But today is a big day for the police. An infamous criminal has been arrested. Her real name is as yet unknown, but she is called the Dark Angel."

Mika can see Mr. Douglas stiffen. Then he regains his cool and takes a sip from his glass. "You don't say."

The chair creaks from Valdemar's weight when he leans back and blows a cloud of smoke toward the ceiling.

"Among the Dark Angel's belongings was a ledger of clients who have used her services. It might surprise you how many high society families were on that list."

"No, I mean, yes, we would surely be surprised," Mr. Douglas says quickly. "We have never heard of the person in question, right, Marianne?"

"Certainly not," Mrs. Douglas agrees, a slight but obvious tremble in her voice.

"Of course you haven't," Valdemar says. "If you had, my visit here would have looked entirely different. Then I would have been forced to bring you out in handcuffs in front of your servants and your neighbors and all the journalists gathered in the square. It would have been very embarrassing for all involved."

Mr. and Mrs. Douglas exchange a quick look.

"Well, this is not just a social visit," Valdemar continues. "My colleague has a proposition for you."

"Your . . . colleague?" Mr. Douglas says, confused.

Mika steps forward. "My name is Mika, and I work at the Public Children's Home. If you are unable to care for your grandchild, we can help you find a foster home. In that case, I will arrange a meeting with Amelia Ståhl, who is the orphanage houseparent."

Mr. Douglas stares at Mika, then purses his lips. "Certainly not. I can take care of my own grandchild."

Valdemar leans forward and stares at the Douglases.

"I very much hope so," he says, and there is not an ounce of politeness left in his voice, now deeper than the deepest void. "Because if I hear something different, my next visit will not be as pleasant. Then the honor that you are so eager to preserve will be dragged into the gutter and hung up to dry in public, forever."

Not a muscle moves on Mr. Douglas's face. He sits as stiff as a statue, his eyes on the match that has now burnt a hole in the lacquer of the sofa table. Mika notices the glass in Mr. Douglas's hand. At first glance, his grip looks steady, but then she sees tiny ripples spreading across the surface of the cognac.

He is shaking, Mika thinks.

"Beatrice will miss some of her education for the birth, of course," Mika says. "But the school administration will probably be reasonable if you explain the circumstances. The two of you surely understand that Beatrice's quitting school would bring unfortunate consequences not only for her, but for the two of you as well."

Mr. Douglas swallows visibly. Then, without looking up, he nods. Mrs. Douglas opens her mouth to say something but then closes it again.

"That's probably everything," Valdemar says, putting his hat on. "Thank you for the visit. We will show ourselves out."

Mika and Valdemar leave the study and the Douglases remain on the couch behind them, pale and mute.

When they walk through the hallway, Mika notices that the door to Beatrice's room is open. She stops in the doorway and looks inside. Beatrice is sitting on her bed with her hands around her big belly. The window is ajar, and the curtain moves a little in the breeze. On the messy desk, among papers and pens, is the gilded birdcage. The hatch is open and the little finch gone. The two girls look at each other in silence, aware of the fact that they will probably never meet again. Then they give each other a quick nod, and Mika follows Valdemar to the stairs.

Outside, on Blasieholmen Island, the cobblestones are still shiny from the morning rain.

"Did you learn anything?" Mika asks. "About the name, I mean."

"It didn't take too much research," Valdemar says. "As opposed to your mother's family, there are a few families in this city with that same name. But only one of the families has a male who might fit. They live not far from here."

He looks thoughtfully at Mika.

"Certain things might be sensitive, even after many years have passed. Maybe you should wait, figure out if this is really what you want. You could send a letter first."

Mika glares at him, her jaw clenched.

"This is not a fairy tale," she snorts. "And I expect nothing. The only thing I know is that I have waited long enough. I don't have time to send a damn *letter*."

Valdemar gives her a lopsided smile. "I was hoping you'd say that."

CHAPTER 31

At the end of Wahrendorffsgatan, next to Berzelii Park, is a four-story brown stone building. The house is not lifeless, like the Douglases'; several windows are open, and the front door is framed by roses on a vine. From one of the windows comes the sound of somebody playing the piano. Mika has a sudden impulse to turn around, but Valdemar resolutely goes up and knocks on the front door, causing the windowpanes to rattle. After a while, the door is opened by a young maid, only a few years older than Mika. The girl looks happy, but her smile dies when she notices the saber hanging from Valdemar's belt.

"My name is Constable Hoff," Valdemar greets her with authority. "I am looking for Sebastian Gille."

The maid curtsies and steps aside. "Come inside, Constable."

She shows Mika and Valdemar to the sitting room next to the entryway. "You may wait here."

The maid hurries out through another door, and they are alone. In the middle of the sitting room is a group of heavy gilded chairs. Above them hangs a crystal chandelier from a beautiful ceiling rosette. The floor is covered with wall-to-wall rugs, and by the tall windows hang thick red velvet curtains. Everything is so beautiful it makes Mika feel like a burglar. Her stomach cramps and she feels like throwing up. Just as she is about to turn around and rush to the front door, Valdemar puts his hand on her shoulder. He doesn't say anything, just stays like that until she starts breathing normally again.

After a while, the door handle turns, and a man appears. The man has a distinct nose, dark hair that has been combed back, and blue eyes. His gray suit is spot-free and from his vest pocket hangs a heavy gold chain. Mika tries to see herself in him, but she can't. The man in front of her is from another world.

"My name is Sebastian Gille. What can I help you with, Constable?"

Valdemar looks at Mika with his calm eyes. He nods, almost imperceptibly, and steps back.

"I am looking for a person," Mika says. "And I am hoping that you might be able to help me find her."

Sebastian Gille looks at Mika, surprised.

"A person," he repeats. "Who might that be?"

"Her name is Annie Moonwind."

Sebastian Gille tilts his head, as if Mika has asked him a riddle. "And why might you be looking for Annie Moonwind, if I may ask?"

Mika takes a deep breath.

"She is my mother. My name is Mika, and I will be thirteen years old this year."

The room turns silent. The only sound that can be heard is the soft tinkle of a piano somewhere in the building. The truth washes over Sebastian Gille's face like a wave; he stumbles and grabs the back of a chair to steady himself. His eyes look frightened when he looks at Valdemar.

"We are not here on police business," Valdemar says, holding his hands up in a calming gesture. "I am here as Mika's friend and coworker."

Sebastian Gille looks confused but collects himself. "May I ask how you found me?"

"I got your name from somebody who knew my mother," Mika says. "Don't worry. I'm only here to learn my story."

"You have the right to," Sebastian Gille says quietly. "But I don't know if this is the right time."

"It is as right as it can ever be," Valdemar's deep voice says in the background.

Sebastian Gille is quiet for a long time. Then he nods and looks around quickly, as if to make sure they're alone in the room.

"After what happened, my parents insisted that Annie, I mean Miss Moonwind, stop working for the family. They were very firm. But in the end, I managed to persuade them, practically through blackmailing them, to move Miss Moonwind to a family property run by my younger brother, in Morgongåva, outside Uppsala, and allow her to work there. Since then, I have only seen her a few times. As far as I know, she is still there."

As Sebastian Gille takes a breath to continue his story, the door slams open, and a boy rushes in. The boy is around five years old, has the same dark hair as his father, and is dressed in a tidy sailor's suit.

"Who is that?" the boy asks earnestly, pointing at Mika.

"We're busy," says Sebastian Gille brusquely. "Go to your mother immediately."

"My name is Mika," Mika says. "What's your name?"

"Fredrik," the boy replies, sending his father a challenging look.

"What a nice name," Mika says. "And what a nice suit you have."

Fredrik makes a face and pulls demonstratively at the back of his pants. "It's too tight," he says. "But I get to take it off later, when we get a bath."

Mika is seized by an impulse to hug Fredrik. He is her half brother, a beloved boy who gets to take baths and speak his mind. Safe and healthy, he lives his life without hunger or slaps. Mika wants to touch him, just to see how a child like that might feel, if there is a difference.

Then they hear the sound of heels on the floor, and a woman in a green dress with her hair styled on top of her head comes into the room.

"I am so sorry," the woman says. She smiles at Valdemar. "Our Fredrik is a genius at running away from his piano lessons."

"I understand him," Valdemar says with a grin.

The woman ushers her son out of the room. It's obvious that she is curious about the visitors. When the door closes, Sebastian Gille looks at Mika with a serious expression.

"Except for my mother, nobody in the family knows this whole story," he says quietly. "If you—"

"I don't want anything from you," Mika interrupts him. "I just want to know what happened."

Sebastian Gille makes sure that the door is closed all the way before he continues.

"Your mother and I were very much in love; I want you to know that. My father was seriously ill, and I was in line to inherit the business. My parents gave me an ultimatum. Through friends, they got in touch with a woman who got paid to make children disappear. You have probably never heard of her, but in those days she was called the Dark Angel. Annie and I could not let this happen, so we decided to save you. I found a midwife who delivered you in secret and then I handed you over to the children's home. When my parents understood that you were gone, they were furious, and they had Annie committed to Konradsberg, where she stayed for three months before I got her released. In exchange for Annie keeping her job, I agreed to end the relationship and take over the business. Even if we didn't manage to have a life together, there was comfort in knowing that you were in a place where nobody could reach you."

"And it was fine," Mika says. "I survived."

She holds out a hand to Sebastian Gille. "Thank you."

They shake hands. Sebastian Gille's nails are even and clean, Mika notices. The palm of his hand is as soft as the belly of a cat, not rough like her own. Then it hits Mika. Mr. Gille has touched her twice. Almost thirteen years ago, when he dropped her off at the orphanage. And now.

She swallows and steels herself so she can look him in the eye. "You don't need to pay my fee anymore," she says.

Mika drops his hand, turns around, and walks toward the exit. Valdemar follows her without a word. When they near the door, Mika slows down. But the man who is her father doesn't say anything else. The door slams shut behind them and they hear the key turn in the lock.

Mika and Valdemar walk along Wahrendorffsgatan in silence. At the corner of Östra Trädgårdsgatan, Mika throws her arms around Valdemar and buries her face against his stomach. From inside of her rises a childish, loud cry that feels embarrassing but is impossible to stop. Valdemar says nothing; he just puts his heavy arms around her shoulders. When Mika has cried for a while, she lets go.

"There," she croaks and wipes her nose on her shirt-sleeve. "I'm done."

In the middle of Valdemar's shirt is a wet snot spot, but that doesn't seem to bother him. He sticks his hand in his pant pocket and pulls out his snuffbox. Slowly and methodically, Valdemar prepares his wad of snuff while he watches little children showering in the spray from the King's Garden fountain. With his thumb, he pushes the wad in under his lip and wipes his hand on his pants.

"Morgongåva," Valdemar says thoughtfully, as if he is taking a bite out of the word, tasting every syllable. "It sounds like a nice place, doesn't it?"

CHAPTER 32

First, Mika chops a chunk of wood on the small chopping block in the kitchen and puts the logs in the oven. Then she carves a few sticks with the sharp edge of the axe and fits them into the gaps between the bigger logs. She strikes a match against the matchbox and holds the flame to the thin sticks, which immediately catch fire and begin curling from the heat. She carefully blows on the embers until the oxygen makes the flames rise and bite into the wood. When the bark begins to crackle, Mika closes the hatch. She fills a pot with water and puts it on the burner. Then she puts all the cups and plates from lunch into the sink. While she waits for the water to boil, she contemplates her image in the window. The bruises around her neck have paled. On her cheeks and forehead are tiny, red freckles. Those are the marks that she got from the dynamite splatters at the explosion in the Dark Angel's apartment. Mika has always felt older than she is, but now it is obvious that something has changed. It may be her eyes—she is not one of the children anymore. She suddenly sees somebody move in the background and turns around. In the door stands Amelia with a newspaper in her hand.

"They're talking about the Dark Angel today," she says. "Do you want to read it?"

Mika hesitates for a moment, but then she shakes her head. "No."

She remembers the words that the Dark Angel said—that in the end, even the unthinkable can become a habit. Mika doesn't want to live like that. And she never wants to hear about, or even think about, the Dark Angel again.

Amelia puts the newspaper away and pulls the pot off the heat. "That can wait."

She puts a hand on Mika's arm. "Cecilia is here. It's time."

Mika quickly takes off her apron; then she follows Amelia through the hallway to the ward for the younger children. In one of the chairs outside the room, Cecilia sits with Nora in her arms. They both light up when they see Mika.

"We're glad you came back," Amelia says. "I understand that you want to pick up your girl today?"

Cecilia nods.

"I've saved some money, and with the help of my sister I have been able to buy a ticket from a friend who got sick. It's short notice, but I must take this opportunity."

"Ticket?" Mika says, surprised. "Are you going away?"

Cecilia's eyes look both sad and happy at the same time.

"The boat leaves Gothenburg the day after tomorrow," she replies. "The first stop is Hull, England, then we take the train to Southampton, and from there we travel on to America, on a one-way ticket. We're starting a new life, Nora and I, on the other side of the ocean."

"You don't have to flee," Mika protests. "The Dark Angel has been caught. She can't hurt you anymore."

"I am choosing to leave," Cecilia says with determination. "As long as I have been on this earth, I have waited for life to begin. Now I'm doing something about it."

She smiles at Mika. "Do you want to hold her?"

Mika sits in the easy chair and, when she takes Nora, she remembers the previous winter when Nora was dropped off at the orphanage, newborn and thin as a twig of a birch tree. Now she is standing up in Mika's lap, a little wobbly in the knees, but strong and healthy. Nora pinches Mika's nose and pulls at her dirty hair. Then she lets out a holler, grabs a firm hold of Mika's ears, and puts her face next to Mika's.

"Goodbye, Nora," Mika whispers against the soft neck, breathing in Nora's smell so she will remember it forever.

Nora has nothing to pack, and as quickly as she arrived at the orphanage, she is gone.

Amelia lingers outside the room afterward. She clearly has something to say. Finally, she does.

"I have asked Lina to help with the younger children for now. She has matured this year and I think the responsibility will be good for her."

Mika nods. "I think so too."

They sit together for a while without saying much more; then Amelia disappears toward the office. Mika isn't sure what to think about Nora moving to America. It feels like she should be sad, but she isn't. Even if she never gets to see Nora again, she is . . . happy. Or almost happy, at least. With a sigh, Mika stands and walks toward the kitchen to deal with the dishes. In the hallway, she meets Rufus, dressed in a shirt and clean pants.

"Are you going to the Chapel today?" Mika asks.

"What's your guess?" Rufus says, and a look of understanding passes between them. "It's payday for the factory workers. The Priest has promised that I'll get some of the tips if I do a good job."

"He always kept my tips," Mika mutters. "Except what ended up in my boots, that is."

Rufus shakes his head and looks almost troubled.

"Lina is helping Amelia, and I'm taking your work at the Chapel. You have almost nothing left to do. What *are* you going to do?"

Mika shrugs. "Whatever I want."

Rufus snorts and rolls his eyes, as if she said something funny.

"I bet you will."

CHAPTER 33

Mika opens her eyes. For a moment she stays in bed, listening to the calm breaths of the children in the dark. Then she swings her legs over the edge of the bed and sneaks soundlessly through the dormitory. At the door, she puts the palm of her hand on the lock to soften the sound of the turning key. She throws a last look at the sleeping bodies in their beds, then carefully closes the door. Stepping lightly, Mika moves through the dark orphanage. She hears the cracking in the walls and the wind swooshing through the chimney, as if the entire building were a sleeping creature. In the kitchen, she lifts the lid of the woodbin where she has hidden the sack with her belongings: two shirts, a pair of extra pants, half a bar of soap, and a sock with three kronor in it. The rest—the brass knuckles and five kronor—she has left for Rufus.

In the entryway, Mika turns around and looks back at the only home she has ever known. For a moment, fear flutters in her stomach. Then she leaves.

Outside, Drottninggatan is dark and deserted. In the sky, the moon is still visible between wisps of clouds, the light of dawn still some time away.

Next to the sidewalk is a carriage with a speckled gelding between the shafts. On the box seat sits a very still figure in a hat and coat.

"Are you alive?" Mika asks.

"Barely," Valdemar says and stretches. "The police force rarely likes to get out of bed before five in the morning, though there are exceptions."

"Poor you," Mika says. "Maybe it will get better after your morning pipe."

"I will save it until we pass Norrtull," Valdemar says, patting his coat pocket. "No fire in the chimney before breakfast."

Then they hear a low humming sound, like a dung beetle. It takes a few moments before Mika understands that it has come from Rutger. He is snoring.

"Will he be able to make it all the way to Uppsala?" she asks.

"We're more alert than we look," Valdemar says, insulted.

Mika laughs and throws her sack in the back. She reaches for Valdemar's hand and her feet lift from the ground; then she lands on the box seat with a thud. Valdemar disengages the brake and gives her the reins.

"We can take turns driving," he says. "But this is your journey; you need to start."

For a moment, Mika sits still and feels the power in her hands. North of Drottninggatan is the deserted area of Siberia with its sheds, then the Ormträsket Swamp, now filled in, then Norrtull and the vast country road. It might as well be the end of the world because Mika has never been farther than this. For the first time, she is about to leave the city where she was born. The familiar fear is there again, like a tiny, sharp rock in her belly. Then Mika sees herself from the outside, sitting on the box seat next to Valdemar, her favorite place in the world. Without thinking, she snaps the reins. Rutger turns his head and gives her a surly glare, then reluctantly starts moving forward. The sense of freedom is immediate and makes her blood fizz like sparkling lemonade. As the carriage rolls by the dark buildings, Mika feels like calling out, as loudly as she can, waking the sleeping city:

My name is Mika Moonwind, and my life is my own!

In the east, the new day glows, though for now it is just a thin strip of light, a promise of what is to come. But what the girl and the man on the box seat can't see is that they have company. Behind them, just enough distance away not to lose sight of the carriage, shuffles a dirty yellow dog with matted fur.

ABOUT THE AUTHOR

Photo © Ylva Sundgren

Johan Rundberg is an award-winning author of children's books who lives in Stockholm. He has written picture books, early readers, and middle grade. In 2021, he was awarded Sweden's most prestigious literary prize, the August Prize, in the children's and YA category for *Nattkorpen*, the original edition of *The Night Raven*, the first book in the Moonwind Mysteries series. *The Night Raven* was a *Kirkus*

Best Book of the Year and was short-listed for the Global Literature in Libraries Initiative Translated YA Book Prize. Both *The Night Raven* and its sequel, *The Queen of Thieves*, were Junior Library Guild selections.

ABOUT THE TRANSLATOR

Eva Apelqvist has been working as a Swedish translator for more than twenty years. She grew up in Sweden and now lives in Minnesota. She recently translated the young adult novel *Fire From the Sky*, written by Moa Backe Åstot, which was named a Printz Honor Book (only the second translated book to have received this honor), was short-listed for the Global Literature in Libraries Initiative Translated YA Book Prize, and was named one of the best young adult books of the year by the Cooperative Children's Book Center. She is also a published children's author in Sweden.